"Until our wedding day I'd never even kissed a guy."

Emmeline dropped her eyes, the admission making her insides squirm with embarrassment. "But when you look at me, it's like...I get it. I get what everyone's talking about. I understand, finally, the appeal of sex. And I don't want to die a virgin."

Pietro couldn't help but laugh softly at the dramatic endnote. "You are not going to die a virgin. You are still young."

"Yes, but...if not now, when? Who?"

An excellent question.

Suddenly the idea of someone else taking this precious gift was anathema to Pietro. The red-blooded man had begun to see his wife as his. Not just a bride of convenience, but a woman under his protection. Was he to let her go, knowing some other man would take what he, Pietro, had so nobly declined?

He groaned softly, knowing then that the devil was on his shoulder and he was listening to his urgings.

"You are too young for me," he said. "And too inexperienced."

One way or another he'd conquer this desire, because nothing and no one ever got the best of Pietro Morelli.

Clare Connelly was raised in small-town Australia among a family of avid readers. She spent much of her childhood up a tree, Harlequin book in hand. Clare is married to her own real-life hero, and they live in a bungalow near the sea with their two children. She is frequently found staring into space—a surefire sign she is in the world of her characters. She has a penchant for French food and ice-cold champagne, and Harlequin novels continue to be her favorite ever books. Writing for Harlequin Presents is a long-held dream. Clare can be contacted via clareconnelly.com or her Facebook page.

Books by Clare Connelly

Harlequin Presents

Innocent in the Billionaire's Bed
Bought for the Billionaire's Revenge

Harlequin Dare

Off Limits

Visit the Author Profile page
at Harlequin.com for more titles.

Clare Connelly

HER WEDDING NIGHT
SURRENDER

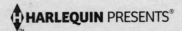

Recycling programs
for this product may
not exist in your area.

ISBN-13: 978-1-335-41929-3

Her Wedding Night Surrender

First North American publication 2018

Copyright © 2018 by Clare Connelly

Printed in U.S.A.

www.Harlequin.com

HER WEDDING NIGHT
SURRENDER

For Kylie Adams, who has supported and encouraged me from the start.

PROLOGUE

'So, LET ME get this straight.' Pietro stared across his desk at the man he'd idolised for the better part of two decades. 'You're actually asking that I marry your daughter—a woman thirteen years my junior, a woman I barely know. And why, exactly, do you suppose I'll say yes?'

Across from him Col shifted in his chair, his own gaze direct. 'Emmeline is a beautiful and intelligent woman. Why are you so offended by my suggestion?'

Pietro's scepticism on that score wasn't something he wished to communicate to his friend. Nor the belief he held that Emmeline was either painfully shy or vapid.

'I have no intention of marrying anyone,' Pietro said, neatly sidestepping the question. 'Ever.'

'Even better. Marrying Emmeline isn't going to skittle any lingering love affair for you.'

Pietro's lips were a gash, scored across his face. He spoke emphatically and with the kind of iron-like command that had his corporate opponents running scared. 'There will be no marriage.'

Col smiled at the swift rebuke. Apparently the commanding tone that Pietro's business adversaries feared was inconsequential to Col.

'I love you, Pietro. Like a son. You and Emmeline are the most important people in my life. I *need* you to marry her.'

'Why? Where has this come from?' Pietro leaned forward, analysing every flicker of the older man's face.

'I've been thinking about it for a few weeks.'

'Why?' Pietro pushed, certain now that he wasn't seeing the full picture.

Col exhaled slowly and his eyes dropped away from Pietro's. 'Emmeline wants to go to university. She's found a place in Rome. I've told her she may come here to study, with my blessing. But only so long as she marries you.'

'And she has agreed?' Pietro snapped scathingly, his impression of Emmeline as a limpet who'd signed her life away on a dotted line increasing.

'It took some discussion,' Col admitted gruffly. 'But, yes, she agreed.' His eyes held a defiant glint in their depths. 'Emmeline would do anything I ask of her. She's always been a good girl.'

A good girl? Pietro had to concentrate hard to stop himself rolling his eyes. Good girls were boring. Predictable. Dull. The description served only to reinforce his dim opinion of the Senator's daughter.

'So?' Pietro laughed, the sound rich with disbelief. 'I can keep an eye on your daughter without marrying her!'

'Damn it!' Col shouted, the words an angry curse on his lips. 'That's not enough.'

'Why not?' Pietro narrowed his eyes. 'What am I missing?'

Col's glare was defiant, his expression rich with displeasure. But after a burning moment of silence he nodded. Just once, but it was enough to signal a surrender of sorts.

'What I'm about to tell you stays in this room.'

Perplexed, Pietro jerked his head in agreement.

'Swear it, Pietro. Swear you will keep my confidence.'

'Of course.'

Pietro had no concept of what he was agreeing to, at that point, so it was easy to go along with the Senator's insistence.

'There are only two people other than myself who know what I'm about to tell you. Not even Emmeline knows.'

A *frisson* of anticipation drummed along Pietro's spine. He stayed silent, waiting for the Senator to continue.

'There's no easy way to say this. I'm dying.'

Pietro froze. He felt his body go into a kind of shocked stasis. 'What?' he heard himself query after a long moment, and the word was almost sucked out of him.

'Dying. My oncologist thinks I've probably got a few months in me yet.'

He leaned forward, and the determination in his gaze sent shivers running down Pietro's spine.

'They won't be *good* months, though. I want Emmeline as far away from me as possible. I want her happy. Safe. Protected. I want her blissfully unaware of what's happening to me.'

Pietro felt as though a slab of bricks had landed on his chest and was determinedly squeezing all the air out of him. He'd lost his own beloved father to cancer twenty years earlier. The idea of going through that again turned his blood to ice.

'That can't be right.' He ran a palm over his eyes and stared at the Senator with renewed interest. He looked so well. Just as always. 'Have you had a second opinion?'

'Don't need one.' Col shrugged. 'I saw the X-rays. Cancer everywhere.'

Pietro swore in his own tongue. It had been a long time since he'd felt so powerless. 'I'm sorry.'

'I don't want your apology. I want your help. Damn it, I'm *begging* you for it.'

Inwardly, Pietro groaned. He would do almost anything for the older man. But marrying his daughter...?

'Surely Emmeline would prefer to find her own partner...'

'Who?' Col scoffed. 'Some fortune-hunter? She's going to be worth billions of dollars when I die. *Billions*. Not to mention inheriting the estate and the oil rig off Texas. And she's got no experience with the world.' He grunted angrily. 'That's *my* fault. After her mother died I wanted to protect her. I wanted to keep her away from all that was ugly. I did a damned good job. But now I find myself with a twenty-two-year-old daughter who's about to be orphaned—and, hell, Pietro, I need to know that someone will look after her.'

'I will,' he assured Col, meaning it.

'The occasional email won't cut it. I need her living under your roof. Emmeline *needs* looking after.'

'You say she doesn't know about the cancer?'

'Absolutely not. And she's not going to.'

'What are you talking about?'

'I want to spare her this pain. I owe her that much.'

Pietro felt frustration gnawing through him. Of all the requests he'd expected, this was nowhere on the list he'd prepared.

'It's the only thing I've ever asked of you, Pietro. Promise me you'll do this. For *me*.'

CHAPTER ONE

'You don't like me, do you?'

She regarded the handsome Italian thoughtfully, taking in his expensive suit, thick dark hair, dark chestnut eyes and lips that looked as if they were made to curse and kiss. Lower, there was the cleft in his chin, then broad shoulders and a muscled chest. Yes, even though he was wearing that suit she knew it would be muscled. There wasn't an ounce of spare flesh on him—just toned, honed body.

A shiver ran down her spine as she wondered just how the hell she was going to go through with this.

Marriage to this man? Talk about a baptism of fire. No experience—and she had very little anyway—could have prepared her for this.

He didn't answer. Had he even heard? She'd asked the question quietly, in a sort of stage whisper.

She sucked in a breath and focussed on him anew. 'I said—'

'I know what you said.'

His voice was accented. Thick with spiced consonants and mystery. He drummed his fingers—long fingers, with neat nails and a sprinkling of hair over the knuckles—on the arm of his chair.

'It's late. Would you like a coffee? Something stronger?'

Emmeline shook her head and her hair, which was long and lay flat down her back, moved a little, like a shimmering curtain. 'I'm fine.'

He compressed his lips and stood, moving across the room with a stride that spoke of raw, feral power. She watched as he took the glass lid off a decanter and tilted it, filling a round highball tumbler with amber liquid. He threw at least half of it back in one go and then spun the glass in his hand, his fingers moving easily around its circumference as he rotated it purposefully.

'I know this all seems crazy...' Emmeline murmured, her eyes large as they found his.

The force of meeting his gaze startled her and she looked away again just as quickly.

His lips curled in an expression of derisive acknowledgement. *'Un po,'* he agreed. 'A little.'

'The thing is, I don't want to upset my father. I've never been able to bear the idea of hurting him.'

Her eyes flicked to his again, and this time she held his gaze, forcing herself to be brave. If she wanted this man to be part of her plan, her bid for freedom, then she needed him to know she wasn't afraid. Even though the charcoal depths of his eyes made her stomach flip and churn, she kept her courage.

'Since my mother died he's wrapped me up in cotton wool. And I've let him.'

She bit down into her lower lip. Contrary to his first impression, it was a full, pleasingly shaped lip, Pietro realised distractedly, before throwing back another measure of Scotch.

Emmeline's sigh was a soft exhalation. 'I've felt for years that I should assert myself more. That I should insist on the freedoms and privileges that any other person my age would have.'

'So? Why have you not?'

For Pietro's part, the very idea of Emmeline's rarefied existence was abhorrent. Virtually from infancy he had bucked against restraint of any kind. He had always wanted more of everything—particularly independence and maturity.

'It's hard to explain.' *Even to herself!*

She had struggled for years to come to terms with the life she was leading—*choosing* to lead, in many ways.

'After Mom's suicide he fell apart. Keeping me safe, knowing I was protected—it became an obsession for him. I couldn't bear to see him hurt again like he was when she died.'

Pietro froze, his body stiff, his expression unknowingly wary. The expression in Emmeline's face touched something deep inside him, tilting him way off balance.

'Yes,' she said, answering his unspoken question, interpreting his silence only as surprise. 'I do know how she died.'

Her face drained of colour and she crossed her slender legs in the opposite direction, her hands neatly clasped in her lap.

'Your father went to great lengths to...to protect you from the truth.'

'Yes.' Her smile was twisted, lop-sided. 'I just told you—protecting me from *everything* has become somewhat of an obsession to him.'

When had Emmeline come to realise that her father's protection was hurting her? That his well-intentioned benevolence was making her miss out on so much in life?

'How did you find out?'

The gravelled question dragged her back to their conversation, and to a dark time in her life that she tried her hardest not to think about.

'I was fifteen—not five,' she said with a lift of her shoulders, her expression carefully neutral. 'He wrapped me up as best he could, but I still went to school and kids can be pretty brutal. She drove into a tree, sure—but it was no accident.'

Her eyes showed all the emotion that her face was concealing. Perhaps under normal circumstances he might have comforted her. But these weren't normal circumstances and she wasn't a normal woman. She was to be his bride, if he agreed to go along with this.

As if he had any choice! The loyalty and affection he felt for Col, combined with the older man's terminal diagnosis, presented him with a black and white scenario.

'I don't think he ever got over losing her, and he's terrified of something happening to me. As much as this all seems crazy, I can see why he feels as he does.' She cleared her throat. This next part was where she really had to be strong. 'So, yes. I think we *should* get married.'

The laugh that escaped his lips was a short, sharp sound of reproach. 'You don't think I'm the kind of man who'd like to ask that question myself?'

'Oh…'

Her eyes narrowed speculatively and there was a direct confidence in her gaze that unsettled him slightly.

'I think you're the kind of man who has no intention of asking that question *ever*. Of *anyone*.' She cleared her throat again. 'If the gossip pages are to be believed, you're more interested in installing a revolving door to your bedroom than settling down.'

His smile was laced with icy disdain. 'Is that so?'

'Your…*exploits* are hardly a tightly guarded secret.'

She bit down on her lip again, her eyes dropping to the floor. The lighting was dim, but he could see the flush of pink in her cheeks.

'No,' he agreed softly.

The word should have been a warning, but Emmeline had no experience with men at all. And definitely not with men like Pietro Morelli.

'I don't propose you stop…um…that…' She waved a hand in the air, the dainty bangles she wore jingling like windchimes on the eve of a storm.

'Don't you? My, my—what an accommodating wife you'll be.'

'I won't *really* be your wife,' she pointed out quickly. 'I mean, we'll be married, but it will be just a means to an end. I imagine we can live perfectly separate lives.'

She tilted her head to the side thoughtfully, recalling the details she'd seen of his sprawling mansion on the outskirts of Rome.

'Your house is enormous. We'll probably hardly see one another.'

He rubbed a hand over his stubbled chin, somewhat mollified by her realism in the face of such a ludicrous suggestion. At least she wasn't getting carried away with fairy tale fantasies, imagining herself as a Disney princess and he as her long-awaited Prince Charming.

'And that wouldn't bother you?' he drawled, his eyes raking over her from the top of her bent head to the curved body and crossed legs.

She was the picture of boring, high-society America. No fashion, no sense of style or personality—just a beige trouser suit with a cream blouse and a pearl choker wrapped around her slender, pale neck. Why would *any* twenty-two-year-old choose to style themselves in such a fashion?

'Of course not,' she said, the words showing her surprise. 'I just told you—it wouldn't be a real marriage. My father will be comforted by knowing that we're married—he's so old-fashioned—but I don't think he expects it to be some great big love-match. It's a dynastic marriage, pure and simple.'

'A dynastic marriage?' he heard himself repeat.

'Yes. It's hard for people like us to settle down. To meet a person who's interested in us rather than our fortunes.'

She shrugged her shoulders and Pietro had the impression that Col had been fundamentally wrong about Emmeline. She didn't strike Pietro as particularly vulnerable. If anything, she had an incisive grasp of the situation that he hadn't expected.

'I definitely don't want your money. In fact I don't want anything from you. Just the freedom our marriage offers me.'

Why did that bother him? Her calm insistence that she would take his name and nothing else?

'My mother would like grandchildren,' he was surprised to hear himself say. Baiting her, perhaps? Or trying to unsettle her?

She laughed—a sound that caught him off-guard completely. It was a musical laugh, full of the colour that was otherwise lacking from her.

'She probably already has several, given your reputation.'

Dark colour slashed across his cheeks. 'Are you suggesting I have unacknowledged children running about the place?'

She shrugged. 'Well, I guess it's a possibility you should consider.'

His eyes narrowed thoughtfully. She had more spark than he'd appreciated. It was hidden deep beneath the veneer of cultured, polite society heiress, but her intelligence and acerbic wit were obvious now that he was actually in a conversation with her.

'There aren't,' he said with finality. 'The responsibility of parenthood is not one I would abandon.'

Yes, she could tell that about this man. He had a sombre, ultra-responsible air.

'Then your mother may have to live with disappointment. At least she'll have the satisfaction of not seeing her son in the society pages for all the wrong reasons every weekend.'

She stood up, pacing across the room thoughtfully, reminding him powerfully of his own back and forth with Col earlier that same evening.

'You would need to be far more discreet, though. I'm not marrying you just to be embarrassed or ashamed. The outside world would have to think it was a normal marriage. I suppose we'd have to attend some events together, be seen out in public from time to time—that kind of thing. But within the walls of your home you can do what you want and with whom.'

'So if you were to walk into this room and find me having sex with one of my lovers you would not be concerned?'

Her heart *kerthunked* but she kept her expression neutral. 'Only from a sanitation perspective.'

He bit back a smile at her prim response. 'I see.'

'Daddy seems to think a quick wedding is for the best, and if we were to get married within the month I'd have time to enrol in a couple of subjects for next semester…'

'Subjects?' he asked, a frown marring his handsome face for a moment. Then he remembered her plans to study in Rome. The revelation of Col's cancer had thrown everything else from his mind, particularly Emmeline's reasons for pursuing this marriage.

'Yes. University. I presumed Dad told you?'

'He did,' Pietro agreed.

'Well, then, you see? I'm not going to be in your hair. I'll be out doing my own thing much of the time.'

'And there we may have a problem,' he said thoughtfully. 'While I appreciate your generosity in agreeing that my social life shouldn't be disrupted, I would have no such tolerance for you in return.'

Emmeline tilted her head to one side, her eyes meeting his with obvious confusion. 'What do you mean?'

'I won't marry a woman who wants to go out with other men. Who wants to sleep with other men.'

Emmeline pulled a face full of surprise. The possibility hadn't even occurred to her, but his hard-line stance wrought instant confusion. 'Why not?'

His eyes narrowed dangerously. 'Because it might create the impression that I can't satisfy my wife.'

'Oh, heaven forbid anyone should cast aspersions on your big macho libido,' she said, with a roll of her caramel eyes.

'That is a deal-breaker for me, *cara*.'

She darted her tongue out and licked her lower lip. She hadn't planned to go out looking for a boyfriend. The thought had really never entered her head. But, as she spoke to him now, the injustice of his being allowed to continue sleeping his way around Rome but having no such opportunity herself seemed manifestly unreasonable.

'Then maybe you should abstain as well,' she murmured, tapping a finger on the side of her mouth.

'That's not a very clever suggestion, is it?'

'Why not? It seems only fair.'

He prowled towards her. Yes, *prowled*. She felt like a bird pinned under a rock, with an enormous growling lion circling her, waiting for his moment of attack.

'Because I like sex,' he said, when he was only a step away from her. 'I am a red-blooded male and it's a part of my life. So if you force me to give up sex with other women that leaves only you…'

He left the rest of the sentence unfinished, hanging in the air between them like a plank she would definitely never walk.

'Okay…okay.' She lifted her hands in surrender, but it was too late to stem the wave of sensations that were besieging her body. 'No sex.' Her voice was thready. 'I mean, sex is fine for *you*.' She closed her eyes softly. 'And I'll talk to you if I meet someone I like…deal?'

He compressed his lips, his eyes studying her face. Her cheeks were flushed, her eyes wide, her lips slightly tremulous. Fascinating. Was that because she was annoyed? Or were more pleasurable emotions fuelling her physical response?

'*Si.*'

She expelled a shaking breath, nodding slowly. 'So we'll get married?'

'There are a few other matters to consider,' he said quietly, the words thickened by emotion.

'Such as?'

'Your appearance.'

She froze, her eyes shocked into clashing with his. Arcs of electricity shimmied and sparked between them. 'You mean how I look?'

His lips twisted into a tight, displeased smile. 'That is generally what a person's appearance means, is it not?'

She nodded, moving further away from him. She needed breathing room if she was going to keep a level head about her—particularly given this subject matter.

'What about it?'

'No one is going to believe I chose to marry you.'

He said it simply. So simply that she believed he hadn't meant to wound her.

'Why not?' She narrowed her eyes, hoping her face wasn't showing the effects of the cruelty his words were lashing her with.

'Because you're nothing like the kind of women I date. And, as you so rightly pointed out, there's more than enough images of me with that kind of woman available to anyone who cares to search for my name on the internet.'

As Emmeline had. And she'd seen glamazon after glamazon in those online images: tall, thin, voluptuous, and all stunning. Pietro Morelli had a 'type', all right.

'I like how I look,' she said, but her mind cursed her for the lie it was. Concealing her body and playing down her looks was a habit that had formed many years earlier, and she wasn't sure she had any desire to revise it.

'It would not take much effort,' he said quietly, his eyes moving over her dispassionately, assessingly.

A distant memory flashed before him of the first

time he'd seen her, and the quick, instinctive desire that had warmed his blood before he'd remembered how young she was. She was naturally beautiful; why did she hide her looks?

Fire and outrage burned in her blood. 'No.'

He compressed his lips, hiding the amusement that shifted through him at her determined recalcitrance. 'If I'm going to go through with this I expect you to start dressing as if you actually have a figure and some kind of budget for clothing. It is what people will expect of my wife.'

She stared at him, agog. 'You're joking?'

'No, *carissima*. It's no joke.' His eyes roamed her face analytically. 'This is Roma. Find a boutique and worship your body, then I'll consider it.'

His arrogance and his grim, scathing indictment infuriated her, but the realisation of her dream, the closeness of her escape were things so close she could smell freedom and liberation and she wasn't going to let her appearance stop her.

Not for the first time, though, she felt the sharp needling of injustice at the lengths she had to go to in order to earn what most people perceived as a God-given right. What if she refused? Refused not just his request that she start to pay attention to her looks but also her father's suggestion that they marry? What if she took a credit card and just ran away?

It wasn't as if she hadn't thought about it. But the thought of what it would do to her father had always brought her swiftly back into line. She couldn't hurt him. But here she had a way to be independent *and* make her father happy. She just had to tick a few boxes along the way.

'Fine.' Determination and resilience still glinted in her eyes.

'Good.' He nodded crisply.

He reached into his pocket and pulled something out. Something small and white. When he handed it to her she saw it was a business card with a woman's name on it: *Elizabetta Ronimi.*

'This is my secretary's number. She will organise the details with you. Any time in the next month is fine for me.'

'You want *me* to organise our wedding?'

He shrugged, as though it didn't matter one bit to him. 'I presumed you'd hire someone to do it, actually, but you'll need to speak to Elizabetta regarding my availability and to co-ordinate your move to my villa. *Si?*'

'*Si,*' she mumbled wearily. 'I suppose that makes sense.'

'Good.'

She stared at him for several seconds before the penny dropped that she was being dismissed. Colour warmed her cheeks as she moved towards the chair she'd occupied and scooped up her clutch purse.

'I'll have Remi take you home.'

'Remi?'

'My driver.'

'Oh, right.' She nodded, but then shook her head. 'I can grab a cab,' she murmured.

He stopped her on the threshold to the room, his hand curving around her elbow. Warmth spiralled through her body, making her blood pound. Her gut twisted with something like anticipation and her mouth was dry.

'He will soon be your driver too, *cara*. Go with him.'

She didn't want to argue. She wanted to get out of there by the quickest means possible.

'Thank you.'

'Non ce di che,' he said softly. 'See you soon, Mrs Morelli.'

Emmeline's eyes swept shut as she stepped out of his office, one single question pounding through her brain.

What the hell have I just agreed to do?

CHAPTER TWO

THE SUN WAS high in the sky and beating down over Rome, but Emmeline barely felt it. She was cold to the centre of her being, anxiety throbbing through her.

In the end it had taken five weeks to get all the paperwork in order, including a swift visa application for Italy, helped in no small part by the last name that had always opened doors for her.

But who was this woman looking back at her now? She had a growing sense of desperation as she studied her own reflection, doubt tangling in her gut.

'Aren't you glad we went with the Vera?' Sophie asked, wrapping an arm around her best friend's shoulders, her own expression not showing even a hint of doubt. 'You're a vision.'

Emmeline nodded slowly. Sophie was right. The dress was exquisite. A nod to nineteen-twenties glamour, with cap sleeves and a fitted silhouette, its beading was perfect, and the shoes she'd chosen gave her an extra lift of height—not that she needed it.

Her hair had been styled in a similarly vintage look, pulled to one side and curled lightly, then held in place with a diamond clip that had belonged to Grandma Bovington. At her throat she wore a small diamond necklace, and vintage earrings completed the look. Her make-up was the work of some kind of magician, because the woman staring back at Emmeline actually looked...*nice.*

Beautiful?

Yes, beautiful.

'I guess we should get going.'

'Well, yeah, we're a little late—but that's your prerogative on your wedding day, isn't it?'

Emmeline grimaced, lifted her head in a brief nod.

'Honey, you're going to need to work on your happy face,' Sophie said quietly. 'Your dad's never gonna believe this isn't torture for you if you don't cheer up.'

'It's not torture,' she said hastily.

Though she'd kept the truth behind this hasty marriage to herself, Sophie knew Emmeline well enough to put two and two together and get a glaringly clear picture of four.

'It had better not be. I've seen your groom already and—*whoo!*' She made an exaggerated fanning motion across her face. 'He is hotter than a spit roast in hell.'

Emmeline could just imagine. Pietro Morelli on *any* given day of the week was more attractive than a single human being had any right to be, but on his wedding day...? Well, if he'd gone to half the trouble and expense she had then she knew she'd better start bracing herself.

'Suit?'

'Yes. But it's how he wears it!'

Sophie grinned, and it occurred to Emmeline that Sophie was far more the type of Pietro's usual love interest. With silky blonde hair that had been styled into a voluminous bun on the top of her head and in the emerald-green sheath they'd chosen for her bridesmaid's dress, there was no hiding her generous curves in all the right places and legs that went on forever.

Sophie was also a political daughter—though of a congressman rather than a senator—and yet she had a completely different attitude to life and love than Emmeline. She'd always dated freely, travelled wherever and whenever she wanted. For every measure of obsessive attention Col had suffocated Emmeline with, Sophie had been given a corresponding quantity of freedom and benign neglect.

Emmeline had read her emails from Sophie with rapt envy, studying the photographs and closing her eyes, imagining herself alongside her friend. What had Paris on a spring evening smelled like? And how had Argentina been in the summer? And what about that time she'd travelled on a yacht around the Mediterranean, stopping in the French Riviera for a month just because it had taken her fancy?

But all that was ahead of Emmeline now. Soon it would be *her*!

This marriage was crazy in no small part, but it was also the smartest thing she'd ever done. Marriage to Pietro was freedom—freedom to live her own life without hurting her father. Freedom to explore, travel, to *live*—away from Annersty and yet not carrying the burden of having let her father down.

Was there any other way? A way that would give her *true* freedom? The kind of freedom that *wasn't* purchased by marriage? The freedom of knowing she could live her own life?

She bit down on her lower lip, her eyes unknowingly haunted. Of course there was. She could have packed a bag and announced that she was leaving home at any time.

So why hadn't she? Because she'd been with her father when her mother had died. She'd seen the way it had killed a part of his heart, withered it forever, and she didn't dare do the same to him. She couldn't hurt him.

She was making the right decision. She'd get what she wanted, albeit in a not particularly easy way, and her father would be placated. And then, eventually, she'd divorce Pietro and all would be well.

A renewed glint of determination shifted through her eyes. 'Let's go.'

Sophie nodded her approval. 'Attagirl. That's better.'

She sashayed to the door of the small room at the back of the ancient chapel, craning her head out and nodding.

Music began to play—loud and beautiful. A mix of organ, strings and woodwind. It was Pachelbel's *Canon in D*, a piece that Emmeline had always loved.

She watched as Sophie disappeared ahead of her, counted the ten seconds Maria her wedding co-ordinator had advised and then stepped out of the anteroom into the back of the chapel.

It was packed. The pews were crammed full of well-dressed guests. Many of her father's political friends had come, a few of her schoolfriends, and apparently all of Italy's upper echelons of society had turned out to get a look at the woman who'd finally brought renowned bachelor and commitment-phobe Pietro Morelli to his knees.

She moved along the back of the church, behind the last row of guests, smiling as she caught the eye of someone she vaguely remembered having met once or twice on her visits to the Capitol.

The smile clung to her lips as she saw her father waiting for her. His eyes were moist with unshed tears, his body slim and lean in a fine suit. He wrapped her in a bear hug, almost squashing her, and then kissed her cheek.

His eyes, when he pulled back, searched hers. 'Ready?'

She nodded, smiling brightly at him. She wouldn't let him think she had doubts. Having agreed to this, she wouldn't let him live with any kind of guilt over the fact that he'd pressured her into marrying a man she didn't know—a man called Pietro Morelli, no less!

'Good.' He nodded. 'I'm glad.'

He turned his body slightly and she turned with him, towards the front of the church. She looked past the acres and acres of guests, standing and staring with undisguised curiosity, and there was her groom.

Oh, boy.

Sophie really hadn't been exaggerating. In fact she might have waxed a little more lyrical about just how freaking gorgeous her groom looked. *All other Italian pin-ups—eat your heart out.*

His skin was darker than it had been a few weeks ago, as though he'd been out in the sun a lot. Emmeline tried not to imagine him sunbaking on the Riviera, with a suitably gorgeous companion all too willing to rub oil over his body. Was it an all-over tan? Of course he'd have a private spot to go around in the altogether...

Her father was walking, and she had no choice but to walk with him. One foot in front of the other. But as she got closer her trepidation doubled. Up close to Pietro, she was reminded powerfully of that handsome face with its permanent scowl and the dark, intelligent eyes, his chiselled jaw and symmetrical features. The broad body that she somehow just *knew* would be hard and warm.

His eyes met hers and there was something in them—challenge? Admiration? No, not that. But his look was intent. He stared at her long and slow, uncaring of the hundreds of guests assembled, nor the priest who was waiting patiently.

Col extended a hand and Pietro shook it. This evidence of their firm, long-held friendship gave Emmeline a much-needed boost. A timely reminder that he wasn't a wolf—well, not *just* a wolf. He was someone who had every reason and every intention to be just what they'd agreed. A convenient husband. He was simply a very handsome means to a definitely necessary end.

'*Cara,*' he murmured, low and deep, in a husky greeting that set her pulse firing and spread goosebumps over her flesh. He leaned in close, whispering to her through the veil that covered her face. 'This is more like it.'

Her heart turned over at the compliment, but something like impatience groaned in her chest—impatience that he might think she'd gone to all this effort for *him*; impatience at the fact that he was right.

She arched a brow and met his eyes without showing a hint of her turmoil. 'I thought about wearing a suit, but, you know… This seemed more appropriate.'

'Definitely. I almost wish I was going to be the one to remove it.' He straightened, the hit having met its mark.

Her cheeks glowed with warm embarrassment at his comment, and the effect it had had on her body.

Traitorous flesh.

Her nipples peaked, straining against the soft fabric of her bodice, and an image of him doing just that spooked into her mind. His suit would be rumpled, his jacket discarded, the tie gone, the shirt half unbuttoned with its sleeves pushed up to expose his tanned forearms. There were seemingly a thousand buttons on her dress—probably actually only fifty—and it had taken Sophie the better part of a half-hour to pull the dress together. Would he move slowly or quickly?

She swallowed, staring straight ahead.

The service itself was surprisingly swift. A simple recitation of vows, just as she'd seen in dozens of movies and television shows, preceded by the question about whether or not anyone objected.

That part had had Emmeline holding her breath, waiting, wondering—and strangely hoping no one would say *Yes, this is a sham!* She'd waited, watching intently as the priest's eyes had skimmed over the congregation.

Finally he turned to the couple, smiling brightly.

'Then without further ado, I now pronounce you man and wife.'

Not *husband* and wife, she noted in the small part of her brain still capable of rational thought. 'Husband' and wife would suggest that he too had been altered in some significant way by what they'd just done. 'Man' and wife made all the changes hers.

'You may now kiss your bride.'

She winced unknowingly. *Your* bride. A possessive phrase that spoke of ownership and rankled. Well, what had she expected? She'd chosen this path to freedom because it was easy. Because it meant she wouldn't have to upset her father. She deserved to feel a little objectified.

Her small facial expression of displeasure was easy for Pietro to discern. Seeing it pass across her face like a storm cloud, he wrapped an arm around her waist, drawing her closer to his body quickly, easily, giving her no chance to question his actions. His eyes briefly met hers and there was sardonic amusement at the heart of his gaze.

She tilted her chin defiantly, inadvertently giving him the perfect angle of access. He dropped his lips to hers, pressing them against her mouth, separating her lips easily and sliding his tongue inside.

It was an invasion of every single one of her senses.

Did he know it was her first kiss? Yes, her first kiss—at the age of twenty-two and on her wedding day. Shame made her toes curl and yet desire heated her up, right to the base of her abdomen. His fingers on her back feathered across her nerve-endings, and she made a small whimper low in her throat that only her groom could possibly have heard.

He broke the kiss, his eyes meeting hers laughingly.

Was he laughing at her?

Her heart was racing, banging against her ribs so hard she thought it might crack them. Her breath was burning inside her body and she stared at him in a tangle of confusion. It took at least ten seconds for her to remember where she was and who she was with.

'I would slap you if all these people weren't watching us,' she muttered under her breath, pasting a tight smile to her face.

His lip lifted in sardonic mockery. 'Or would you rip my clothes off?' he pondered.

But before she could respond, he reached down and took her hand in his.

'They *are* watching, so keep pretending this is the happiest day of your life.'

By the time they'd reached the end of the aisle, having paused several times to accept good wishes and hugs of congratulation, Emmeline's mouth was aching from the forced smile she'd adopted.

A crowd had formed beyond the church and there was a throng of paparazzi. Inwardly, Emmeline trembled at the idea of being photographed. Her husband apparently had no such qualms.

'Ready?' he asked, pausing just inside the door, sparing a quick glance at her face.

Then again, why *would* he hesitate? This was his life. If the number of photographs of him on the internet proved anything it was that he was followed and snapped often. He probably couldn't walk down the street without someone taking his picture.

But Emmeline's life hadn't been like that. A handful of society events had led to her picture sometimes being splashed in the papers, though not often. She was too drab. Boring. Ugly. Why print a picture of Emmeline Bovington unless it was to compare her unfavourably to the renowned beauty her mother had been?

She closed her eyes, sucking in a deep breath, and was unaware of the way Pietro's eyes had caught the deceptive action.

He studied her thoughtfully. He'd seen panic before, and he saw it now. Was this idea *so* unpalatable to her? Hell, she'd suggested it and her father had railroaded him. If anyone should be panicking it was Pietro.

Her hesitation annoyed him—probably more than it

should. He stepped out through the door, holding her hand and bringing her with him into the brightness of the Italian afternoon. The steps towards the street were empty, but beneath them was a large crowd, and as they erupted from the church applause broke out. Rose petals were thrown high into the air. The noise was deafening.

He smiled, lifting a hand in acknowledgement, and turned towards his bride.

There it was again.

Panic.

Blinding, devastating panic.

Impatience crumpled his common sense and quickly ate up his judgement. He caught her around the waist and this time he tipped her back in a swoon worthy of an old black and white Hollywood movie.

His lips on hers were an assault; it was a kiss that gave voice to his annoyance when he wasn't otherwise able to. Her hands curled around his neck, her fingers tangling in the hair at his neck, and she made that noise again. That little whimper of confusion that made him hard all over.

That annoyed him even more, and he pressed his hands into her back, lifting her higher, pressing his arousal against her abdomen, leaving her in little doubt of just what kind of man she'd married.

It lasted only seconds, but when he eased her back to stand and pulled away from her the crowd broke out into thunderous applause.

Her eyes were thunderous too. Thunderously pissed off. He could practically hear the storm brewing.

Good. Let Little Miss Refined work on *that*.

'I swear to God, kiss me again and I'll wait until you're asleep and do some serious damage to you,' she said angrily, but her smile was plastered on again seconds later as Col came up behind them.

'I know I wanted this for you both, but seeing you together…' He shook his head wistfully, tears in his eyes. 'I could die a happy man right now.'

Emmeline laughed, not noticing the way her husband had stiffened at her side. 'God, Daddy, don't say that. You'll tempt the heavens.'

'*Che sera, sera,*' Col said with a shrug.

Emmeline dismissed that attitude. Her father was clearly thrilled that the wedding had taken place, and she wasn't going to take that away from him. Now there were several family photographs to pose for.

Emmeline had met Pietro's mother Ria a few times over the years, and it was easy enough to make conversation with her. His brother Rafe was similarly easy. At least five years younger, Emmeline wondered why *he* hadn't been suggested as a possible groom by her father. He boasted the same pedigree and was equally handsome. Less established in his career, it was true, but with their family fortune what did that matter?

'So, you're now my sister-in-law, eh?'

She returned Rafe's smile, and felt herself relaxing as they posed in the sunshine for the requisite shots.

Nonetheless, it was a relief when the photographer declared she had enough 'for now' and they were free to return to their guests. For Emmeline, that meant Sophie and a hint of normality.

'Ah, the woman of the hour.' Sophie grinned, passing her half-finished champagne flute to Emmeline.

'Don't remind me.' She took a sip, and then another, closing her eyes as the cold bubbles washed down her throat.

'So, Maria was just running through the details with me.'

'Ugh—there's still more, isn't there?'

Sophie laughed softly. 'The reception. But don't worry—that's just a cocktail party at a gorgeous restaurant overlooking the river.'

'Okay, I can cope with that.'

'Then you and Pietro will take your leave—insert catcalling and whistling—and the rest of us young, hip and happening people will have an open bar at some club that's just opened. Apparently your husband had something to do with the financing of it.' Sophie shrugged. 'Sounds kind of fun.'

Emmeline pulled a face. 'Not to me. I can't think of anything worse.'

'Yes, well… I'm sure you'll have your hands full anyway…'

Emmeline sent her friend a scathing look. 'Yeah, right.'

'Hmm, I saw the way you guys kissed. I know passion when I see it.'

Emmeline practically choked on her champagne. She coughed to cover it, lifting a hand to her mouth.

'Trust me—that's not what this is.'

'Then you need to get to a hospital, because if you can be in the same room as that guy and not need CPR then you are some kind of cold fish.'

'Or just a very sensible woman,' she said quietly.

The formalities seemed to last forever. Speeches. The cutting of the cake. Their first dance as a couple…

Emmeline stood in Pietro's arms, trying her hardest to pretend not to be affected by her husband's touch when a single look had the power to turn her blood to lava.

'So…' he drawled, the single word imbued with more cynicism than she'd known was possible. 'You are my wife.'

The sentence brought a smile to her face, but it wasn't a smile of pleasure.

'Don't sound so thrilled about it.'

He slowed the movement of their bodies, his eyes scanning the crowd. 'I can name three people who are beside themselves,' he said coldly.

She followed the direction of his gaze. Her father and his mother stood to one side, each of them beaming with obvious pleasure.

'Yeah, I guess this is a dream come true for Daddy,' she said with a small shake of her head.

There was a look of frustration in her eyes that Pietro thought about probing. But the last thing he wanted was to get to know his inconvenient bride any better.

'And for my mother,' he said simply. 'I'm sure she's imagining a lifetime of calm now that I've apparently hung up my bachelor shoes.'

'Apparently.' She repeated the word, rolling it around in her mouth, wondering about the practicalities of what they'd agreed to. The idea that he'd be free to see other women so long as he was discreet.

It didn't bother her. At least that was what Emmeline told herself. And yet a pervasive sense of confusion filled her.

They would be living under the same roof, seeing each other in the hallways, the kitchen, the lounge, the pool. Despite her protestation that they'd be like flatmates, was it possible that she would be able to ignore her husband at such close quarters?

From the first moment she'd seen him she'd found him worryingly distracting, and the years hadn't stilled that awareness.

And now they were married...

'You are as stiff as a board,' he complained. 'Did you never learn to dance?'

Her cheeks flushed pink and the look she cast him was laced with hurt. 'I was lost in thought,' she mumbled, making an effort to pay attention to her husband.

'Dancing does not require your mind. It is something you feel in your body. It is a seduction.'

He rolled his hips and colour darkened her cheekbones. His body was every bit as fascinating as she'd imagined. All hard edges and planes, strong and dominating, tempting and forbidden in equal measure.

It would be playing with fire ever to touch him in earnest. This was different—a dance at their wedding was unavoidable. But Emmeline had to keep her distance or she'd risk treading a very dangerous path.

'Relax,' he murmured, dropping his head towards hers. 'Or I will kiss whatever it is you are thinking out of your mind.'

She started, losing her footing altogether. She might have fallen if he hadn't wrapped his arms more tightly around her waist, bringing her dangerously close to his body.

'Don't you dare,' she snapped.

His laugh was like gasoline to a naked flame.

'Then smile. Relax. At least pretend you are enjoying yourself.' He dropped his mouth to her ear and whispered, 'Everyone is watching us, you know.'

She swallowed, her eyes scanning the room over his shoulder. The room was indeed full of wedding guests dressed in beautiful clothes, all smiling and nodding as he spun her around the dance floor.

Emmeline's heart sank.

Pretending to be married to Pietro Morelli was going to require a hell of a lot more patience and performance than she'd envisaged.

It was late in the night and Emmeline stifled another yawn. Sophie had found a group of friends—as always—and was charming them with her wit and hilarity. Emmeline listened, laughing occasionally, though she knew all the stories so well they might as well have been her own. Still, sitting with Sophie and pretending to laugh at her hijinks was better than watching her husband.

Her eyes lifted in his direction unconsciously.

He was still talking to her. The redhead.

Emmeline's frown was instinctive—a response to the visual stimulus of seeing a stunning woman so close to the man she, Emmeline, had married only hours earlier.

The woman had auburn hair that tumbled down her back in wild disarray, and she was short and curvaceous, but not plump. Just the perfect kind of curvy—all enormous rounded boobs and butt, tiny waist and lean legs. Her skin was honey-coloured and her lips were painted bright red. Her nails, too. She wore a cream dress—wasn't it considered bad manners to wear white to someone else's wedding?—and gold shoes.

Who *was* she?

Pietro leaned closer, his lips moving as he whispered in the woman's ear, and the woman nodded, lifting a hand to his chest as she dragged her eyes higher, meeting his. From all the way across the room Emmeline could feel the sexual tension between them.

She stood without thinking, her eyes meeting Sophie's apologetically. *I'll be right back,* she mouthed.

Sophie barely missed a beat. She carried on with the story of the time she'd got caught flying from Thailand to London with very illegal monkey droppings in her handbag—she'd been sold them at a market and told they would bring good luck...whoops!—and Emmeline walked deliberately across the room towards her groom and the woman she could only presume to be a lover—past or future. She didn't know, and she told herself she definitely didn't care.

She was only a step away when Pietro shifted his attention from the redhead, his eyes meeting Emmeline's almost as though he didn't recognise her at first. And then his slow-dawning expression of comprehension was followed by a flash of irritation.

He took a small step away from the other woman, his face once more unreadable.

'Emmeline,' he murmured.

'Pietro.' Her eyes didn't so much as flicker towards the woman by his side. 'I need you a moment.'

His lips twitched—with amusement or annoyance, she couldn't have said. He walked towards her, putting a hand in the small of her back and guiding her to the dance floor.

Before she could guess his intentions he spun her around, dragging her into his arms and moving his hips. Dancing. Yes, he was dancing. *Again.*

She stayed perfectly still, her face showing confusion. 'I don't want to dance any more.'

'No, but you want to speak to me. It is easier to do that if we dance. So dance.'

'I...' Emmeline shook her head. 'No.'

He slowed his movements and stared at her for a long, hard second. 'Why not?'

'Because it's not my...thing,' she mumbled, looking away.

Mortification filled her. So many things she'd never really done. Experiences she'd blindly accepted that she would never enjoy. She'd made her peace with that. But now, surrounded by so many people who'd all lived with such freedoms as a matter of course, wasn't it natural that she was beginning to resent the strictures of her upbringing?

Her voice was a whisper when she added, 'As you so wisely pointed out.'

'Then let me show you,' he said.

And his hands around her waist were strong and insistent, so that her body moved of its own accord. No, not of its own accord; she was a puppet and he her master.

Just as she remembered—just as she'd felt hours earlier—every bit of him was firm. His chest felt as if it was cast from stone. He was warm too, and up close like this she could smell his masculine fragrance. It was doing odd flip-floppy things to her gut.

'You told me you'd be discreet,' Emmeline said, trying desperately to salvage her brain from the ruins of her mind. 'But you looked like you were about to start making out with that woman a moment ago.'

'Bianca?' he said, looking over his shoulder towards the redhead. Her eyes were on them. And her eyes were *not* happy. 'She's a...a friend.'

'Yeah, I can see that,' Emmeline responded, wishing she wasn't so distracted by the closeness of him, the smell. What was it? Pine? Citrus? *Him?*

'Are you jealous?'

'Yes, absolutely,' she said with a sarcastic heavenwards flick of her eyes. She leaned closer, lowering her voice to a whisper. 'We have a deal. I just don't want our wedding guests to see you with another woman. What you do in *private* is up to you.' She let the words sink in and then stopped moving. 'I'd like to go home now.'

Pietro wasn't used to being ashamed. He was a grown man and he'd lived his own life for a very long time. But something about her calm delivery of the sermon he really did deserve made a kernel of doubt lodge in his chest.

He knew he should apologise. He'd been flirting with Bianca and Emmeline was right: doing that on their wedding day wasn't just stupid, it was downright disrespectful. To his bride, sure, and more importantly to their parents.

He stepped away from her, his expression a mask of cold disdain that covered far less palatable emotions. 'Do you need anything?'

'No.'

'To say goodbye to anyone?'

She looked towards Sophie, enthralling her newfound friends, and shook her head. 'I'd rather just go. *Now.*'

Silence sat between them and she waited, half worried he was going to insist on doing a tour of the room to issue formal farewells.

But after a moment, he nodded. 'Okay. Let's go, then.'

He put a hand on her back but she walked away,

moving ahead of him, making it obvious she didn't need him to guide her from the venue. She'd walk on her own two feet.

She hadn't made this deal with the devil to finally find her freedom only to trade it back for this man.

Emmeline Morelli was her own woman, and seeing her husband fawning all over someone else had simply underscored how important it was for her to remember that.

CHAPTER THREE

SHE'D EXPECTED A LIMOUSINE, but instead Pietro directed her to a low, sexy black Jaguar, parked right at the front of the restaurant.

He reached for the front passenger door, unlocking it at the same time, and Emmeline sat down quickly, stupidly holding her breath for some unknown reason. What did she think would happen if she breathed him in again?

He closed the door with a bang and a moment later was in the driver's seat. The car throbbed to life with a low, stomach-churning purr, and he pulled out into the traffic with the consummate ease of a man who'd grown up in these streets and knew them well.

Silence stretched between them and it was far from comfortable. The car had a manual transmission and required frequent gear changes from the man with his hand curved around the leather gearstick, his strong legs spread wide as he revved the engine, his arm moving with the gears.

There was an athleticism in his movements even when simply driving a car.

Emmeline ground her teeth together and focussed on the passing view of starlit Rome. Her new home.

married was dwarfed only by his, and yet he made a decent show of pretending normality.

'I'll show you to your room. Come.'

She thought about making a joke—wasn't it a tradition to carry a bride over the threshold of her new home?—but the tightness of his back as he walked away, the firm angle of his head, showed how little he wanted to laugh about this situation.

Emmeline followed, her gaze wandering over the façade of his house as she went. It was an impressive building. If she had found her host…no, her *husband*… less intimidating she would have asked him a little about it. Still, a place like this had to be in the history books; she could do her own research. Especially once she was at uni and had access to a fantastic library.

She breathed in, imagining the scent of all those books. Renewed purpose reassured her. There was a reason she'd married him. She had to keep that firmly in mind and then all would be well.

'It's late. I won't give you the tour now. Tomorrow the housekeeper will show you where things are.' He stood with his hands in his pockets, his attention focussed squarely ahead.

'That's fine, only…'

'*Si?*' It was an impatient huff.

'Um…where am I supposed to sleep?'

His expression contorted with irritation but he moved forward, down a long corridor, then turned left and took her up a flight of stairs.

'These rooms are for your use.'

He pushed a door inwards, showing her a practical space that had been set up with a desk, a bookshelf and a treadmill. The latter made her smile, though she covered it with a yawn.

'Very good.'

'There is a bathroom through there. And your bedroom is here.'

He nodded towards a third and final door and she turned the handle and pushed the door inwards, her eyes scanning the room with interest.

It was not dissimilar to a particularly lovely five-star hotel. A king-size bed made up with nondescript white bed linen and silvery grey throw cushions, a white armchair near the window and yet another book case, and double doors that presumably concealed a wardrobe.

With increasing interest she stepped into the room, the thick beige carpet soft underfoot.

'No books?' she murmured, eyeing the almost empty shelf. The sole book in its midst was a tourist guide to Rome and she refused to believe its placement had anything to do with her husband. He wasn't thoughtful like that.

'This has been used as guest accommodation in the past,' he said softly. 'The décor is neutral in order to accommodate the guests I've had staying here. You are free to add your own touches—furnish it with whatever books you wish.'

She fluttered her eyelids exaggeratedly. 'Even if I want to paint the walls lime-green?'

His smile was dismissive. 'Your choice. It is not as if I will ever be in here to see it.'

She laughed, but there was a thunderous rolling in her gut that she didn't want to analyse. Anxiety, she told herself. She had taken herself out of the comfiest little nest in the world and dropped herself like a stone into the deep end of a raging river.

'So, hot pink then?' she joked, walking towards the window.

She hadn't noticed at first, but as she got closer she saw that it was in fact French doors, and beyond the window was a small Juliet balcony.

Her heart fluttered as she turned the handle and opened the door, feeling a warm breeze breathe in off the city. They were far enough away that she could make out Rome's landmarks with ease, see their place within the cityscape.

'Your suitcases are in the wardrobe,' he said, definitely impatient now, calling her attention back to the important business of getting settled. 'I wasn't sure if you'd find it invasive for the housekeeper to unpack for you. Let me know if you'd like me to send her up...'

Emmeline waved a hand in the air dismissively. 'I can manage.'

'Fine.' A curt nod. 'My room is down at the other end of the hallway. Last door on the right-hand side. If you need me.'

As in, *Don't bother me unless you're on fire, your room is falling away from the building, and there is no one else you can think of to call.*

'Okay.' She smiled—out of habit rather than happiness.

He paused on the threshold for a moment, his eyes glittering like onyx in his handsome face. *'Buonanotte, cara.'*

'Goodnight.' The word came out as a husky farewell. She cleared her throat but he was gone.

Emmeline stretched her arms over her head and then

moved towards the door to her room, pushing it shut all the way until it clicked in place.

This was her home now.

She shouldn't think of herself as a guest, nor of this arrangement as temporary. She'd married him—for better or for worse—and, while she wasn't stupid enough to imagine they'd stay married forever, this was certainly her place in life for the next little while.

The doors did open on to a wardrobe, as she'd suspected, and her two suitcases sat in the centre. She'd unpack in the morning, she thought, when she had more energy. She pushed one open and pulled out a pair of cotton pyjamas and the prospectus for her university course, putting them on the foot of the bed.

Her feet were aching, her body was weary, her mind was numb. What she needed was a hot shower and the pleasant oblivion of sleep.

She reached around to the back of her dress and groaned out loud. The buttons. The damned *buttons*.

The mirrors in the wardrobe showed exactly what her predicament was. There were what seemed like hundreds of the things; they'd taken Sophie an age to do up, and without help Emmeline would never get out of her dress.

Obviously she could sleep in it. Sure, it was heavy and fitted, and she wouldn't exactly be comfortable, but it would save her any embarrassment and she could simply ask one of the staff to help her the following morning.

Or... a little voice in the back of her mind prompted.

She grimaced. Yes, yes. *Or...*

She pulled the door inwards and peered down the corridor. It was longer than she'd appreciated at first, and somewhere at the end of it was the man she'd married.

Refusing to admit to herself that she was actually a little bit scared, she stepped into the hallway and walked down it, paying scant attention to the artwork that marked the walls at regular intervals. At the end of the corridor she waited outside the last door on the right, taking a moment to ball her courage together.

She lifted her hand and knocked—so timidly that she knew there was no way he would have heard the sound.

Shaking herself, she knocked harder:

Once.

Twice.

Her hand was poised to knock a third time, and then the door seemed to be sucked inwards. Pietro stood on the other side, his face unforgiving of the interruption.

'Yes?' It was short. Frustrated.

'I…' Emmeline swallowed. 'Am I interrupting?'

'Do you need something?'

Her eyes clashed with his—angry gold against unreadable black.

'This is in no way an invitation…'

His lips flickered for the briefest second into a genuine smile. It was so fast she thought she might have imagined it.

'Fine. What is it?'

She spun around, facing the wall of the corridor directly opposite. 'There's a billion buttons and I can't undo them. I guess wedding dresses are designed with the fact in mind that a bride won't be undressing alone…'

'Apparently,' he murmured, moving closer.

She knew that because she could feel him, even though he didn't touch her. His warmth seemed to be wrapping around her like an opportunistic vine up an abandoned wall.

'Would you mind?' she asked quietly, keeping her attention focussed on the bland whiteness of the hall-way wall.

'And if I did?'

'I suppose I could find some scissors somewhere...' she pondered.

'No need.'

And then, even though she'd come to his room for this express purpose, the sensation of his fingertips brushing against her back made her shiver. Her nipples strained against the fabric of her gown in a new and un-expected sensation.

'Are you cold?'

The question caught her off-guard. She bit down on her lip, willing her body to behave, her pulse to quiet, her heart to settle. But her body had its own ideas, and it continued to squirm, delighting in his closeness and his touch.

'I'm fine.'

His laugh was soft, his breath warm. It ran across her back like a wildfire she should have paid better at-tention to.

He pushed at the first button, flicking it open ex-pertly. *One down, nine hundred thousand to go*, she thought bleakly. He dragged his fingers down to the next button and her stomach rolled with awareness.

Emmeline sucked in a deep breath.

He wasn't *trying* to turn her on; this was just how he was. The man oozed sensuality from every pore of his gorgeous, perfectly tempting body.

Still, as he undid the second button and moved on to the third the dress parted an inch at the top, and she was sure it wasn't an accident that his fingertips moved across her skin as he lowered them to button number four.

He worked slowly, and for every second she stood in front of him she felt as if her nerves were being pulled tight, stretched and tormented. At button number twenty he wasn't even halfway down her back, and a fever-pitch of heat was slamming through her.

Had he undone enough for her to take the dress off? She wasn't sure, at this stage, that she much cared if the dress got torn, so long as she could get it off without subjecting herself to another moment of...*this*.

Oh, maybe one more moment, she conceded weakly, sucking in a deep breath as his fingers grazed the flesh near where her bra should be. She hadn't needed one in the dress; its boning was sufficient.

Lower still, and the next two buttons came apart slowly. His fingers were achingly close to her lower back, to the inches of flesh that dipped towards her rear.

No man had ever seen her there, let alone touched her. His fingers lingered on her flesh, not moving downwards, just stroking her skin. Her pulse hammered and her eyes drifted shut on a tidal wave of imagining and longing, on hormonal needs that had long ago been relegated to the back of her mind.

'I... I...' The word stammered out as a dubious whisper. 'I can cope from here,' she said quietly, even though her body screamed in silent rejection of her comment.

He ignored her. His hands moved lower, to the next button, pushing it through its beaded loop, separating the fabric, and then his fingers were back, lingering on the flesh exposed by the undone dress.

'That's enough,' she said again, with more strength

to her words, and she backed them up by moving a step forward, away from him, and slowly turning around.

His eyes almost electrified her. They were full of something—some strange emotion she couldn't process. His jaw was clenched tight and there was displeasure lingering in the harsh curves of his lips.

'Thank you,' she said softly, unaware of how pink her cheeks were, how enormous her pupils, how full her lower lip from the way she'd been savaging it with her teeth.

His eyes dropped to her mouth, and unknowingly she darted her tongue out and licked its edges. His own lips flickered in a small sign that he'd seen the nervous gesture, before his gaze travelled lower, to the curve of her breasts no longer held firm by the dress.

'Did you want to join me, *cara*?' he drawled, those eyes lifting back to hers with something like *knowing* buried in their depths.

She shook her head quickly from side to side, but still she didn't move. Her throat was dry, parched, and it stung as though razorblades had been dragged along it.

'I think you do.'

His smile flickered again, but it was a harsh smile, thoroughly without pleasure.

'I think your nipples are tight and aching for my touch. I think your skin is covered in goosebumps because you want me to kiss you all over. I think you came to me tonight because you're curious about whether sleeping with me would feel like that kiss outside the chapel.'

She stifled a groan. 'But…'

'But?' he prompted, reaching out a hand and capturing hers, lifting it to his lips.

She had expected a kiss, but instead he dug his teeth

into the ball of her thumb and arrows of heat and need shot through her, making her knees shake and her back sway.

She couldn't speak. She could barely think. Sensation and feeling were all that was left in her.

'But you are a virgin?' he prompted, her inexperience not even a question.

Was it emblazoned on her skin somewhere? Like the opposite of a scarlet letter and something only he could see?

'And you are saving yourself for someone you love?' He dropped her hand and let out a harsh sound of laughter. 'Rather a shame, given you've just married *me*.'

His eyes returned to hers with renewed speculation.

'How do women like you even *exist* in this day and age?'

There was anger in the question—an anger she didn't understand.

'Women like me?' She was surprised that her voice came out smooth and calm—cold, even.

'A virgin at twenty-two! Did your father lock you up in some kind of a chastity belt? Build a moat around Annersty?'

Emmeline shook her head. 'Neither.'

'So you just aren't interested in boys? In sex?'

Emmeline grimaced, her cheeks flushing darker. 'I guess not.'

'Your body's reaction to me would dispute that.'

'You're imagining it.'

His laugh was soft. 'Careful, Mrs Morelli. One touch and you melt like butter in my hands. Imagine if I pinned you back against that wall and kissed you as though I wanted so much more from you…'

The image filled her with a sense of strange confusion. She *wanted* him to do that. At least a part of her did. A crazy part. The part that had no pride and no rational ability to think.

'I'm sure I'd be very disappointing after the women you're used to,' she said stiffly, sounding so prim that she cringed inwardly.

He didn't say anything. His hand lifted and reached for the cap sleeve of her wedding dress, and slowly he guided it lower. So slowly that she had plenty of opportunities to say something. To object. But she didn't. She watched him with hooded eyes as he drifted it downwards, the fabric a torment as it pulled over the skin at her décolletage and then lower, exposing one of her breasts to the night air—and to his eyes.

They were neat breasts—not huge. But nor were they tiny—and they were firm. His eyes studied her, but she couldn't tell what he was thinking.

'Has a man ever touched you here?' he asked, the question gravelled.

She shook her head, biting down on her lip.

'Do you want *me* to touch you?'

A slick of moist heat formed between her legs and her eyes were anguished as they met his. She nodded. Just a tiny, almost involuntary movement of her head, accompanied by a mask of abject fear on her face.

He laughed softly, dropping his hands to her waist and yanking her closer. His body was hard all over, and she could feel the hint of his arousal through the fabric of her dress. A moan was thick in her throat.

'And I thought this wasn't an invitation,' he said with sardonic mockery, dropping his head so quickly she couldn't anticipate his intention, moving his mouth over the swell of her nipple and rolling his tongue over its unsuspecting tip.

She cried out at the stark feeling of pleasure. It came out of nowhere and it practically cut her off at the knees. His face was stubbled, and the contrast of his rough chin across her soft breast, and the warm wetness of his mouth, the lashing of his tongue…

She was melting—just as he'd said she would.

Swirling need pounded inside her, creating a vortex of responses she'd never imagined possible. Her body was experiencing its first awakening, and any thought of words or sense had fallen from her mind. There was only this.

She could hear herself mumbling incoherently, needing more than he was giving. A wave was building and she had no idea when and how it would crash. Only knew that it was imperative she stay on it, surf it right to its conclusion.

He dragged his lips higher and she cried out at this abandonment of her nipple. But his hand lifted up and cupped her breast, his thumb and forefinger taking the place of his mouth, twisting and plucking at its sensitised nerve-endings until she was crying out over and over, a fever-pitch of sensation rioting inside her.

His other hand pushed her forward, holding her tight against him as his lips sought hers, kissing her as his hands moved over her, and she cried into his mouth as the feelings became too much, her awareness of him too great.

'Oh, God, please…' she groaned into his mouth, with no idea of what she was asking for, only knowing that she needed *something*. Something he alone could give her.

He pulled away, lifting his head at the same moment as he dropped his hand and stepped backwards. His look was one she couldn't fathom. His chest was moving rapidly, his jaw clenched, but she couldn't understand why he'd stopped. Arousal was a raging river in her bloodstream.

'Go to your room, Emmeline.'

The way he said her name was like warm butter on hot toast. It dripped over her body.

Did he mean *with him*? Was he going to come with her? Her confusion was muddied by the way her body was crying out for him.

'I'm not interested in breaking in virgins.'

He turned away from her, stalking into his own room and picking up the glass of Scotch that was resting on the bedside table.

Her jaw dropped. She stared at him, confused and bereft. 'I'm sorry?'

'No need to apologise,' he said, with a shrug of those broad shoulders.

His hair was tousled. Had *she* done that? Had she run her fingers through it so that it now stood at odd angles, all messy and gorgeous?

'I'm not… I wasn't apologising,' she said, her voice thick with emotion. 'I don't understand why you stopped. I don't—'

His accent was coarse when he was angry. 'I'm not interested in sleeping with you. It would complicate things and undoubtedly be unsatisfying, for me.'

She drew in a harsh breath, her eyes flashing with pain.

'Don't be offended,' he murmured. 'I'm just used to more experienced lovers.'

Mortification curled her toes, flushing away any lingering desire. She spun on her heel, walking quickly down the corridor. It was only when she reached her room that she realised she'd come the whole way with her breast still uncovered.

Pietro stared into his whisky, his expression grim.

That had been a mistake. He could still taste her on his lips, smell her on his clothes, hear her sweet little moans of fierce, hot need as though she were still with him. Worse, he could *feel* her—like a phantom of the night he *could* be having if only he hadn't pulled things to a stop.

He was hungry for her…hard for her.

Col's daughter.

A groan permeated the silence of the room and bounced off the walls, condemning him as it echoed back. He'd married her to save her. He'd married her because he'd felt obliged to help his friend out.

Desiring his wife had never been part of the equation.

And he had to damned well do a better job of remembering that.

CHAPTER FOUR

IT WASN'T AS though she'd lived a particularly active and busy life. Confined to Annersty, her company had been made up predominantly of the staff, her father and the schoolfriends she'd caught up with from time to time for lunch.

But life in the villa was utterly silent.

A week after their wedding, and she'd barely seen her groom.

Thank God! The less she saw him, the less she'd need to remember what a fool she'd been in his arms. What a weak, willing, stupid *idiot*. Shame over that night still had the ability to make her blush.

She wandered further along the citrus grove, reaching up and plucking an orange blossom from a tree as she passed, bringing it to her nose and smelling its sweet fragrance.

Oh, they'd seen each other a few times. Once the next day, when she'd been walking around the villa like a lost lamb having escaped slaughter.

He'd come out of a room which she'd subsequently learned was his home office, full of enough technology to power a spaceship. Their eyes had met and he'd arched a brow—a simple gesture that had conveyed derision and scepticism. She'd dipped her head forward and moved past him, her heart pounding, her cheeks burning, her whole body confounded by mortification.

Two days had passed before she'd seen him again, that time in the evening. He'd walked in through the front door just as she was passing. And he'd looked tired. World-weary. He'd loosened his tie so he could undo his top button, and his jacket had been removed. She'd managed a tight smile and a nod of acknowledgement before she'd scurried away, and even kept her head up as she'd gone.

There were oranges growing in this part of the citrus grove, and further down the gently sloping lawn were lemons and limes. Beyond them were quinces and then olives.

It was a perfect Mediterranean garden—just as she'd always fantasised such a spot would be. She paused at the end of the row, turning around and looking down the hill towards Rome. The sky was streaked with orange and peach: a hint of the sunset that was to follow.

The warmth was quite delicious. She felt it on her skin and smiled. Her first genuine smile since before the wedding.

University would help. She needed activity. Something to do to keep her mind busy. Distracted from *him*. Her husband. And the treacherous way her body had responded to him.

She needed to remember her reasons for embarking on this charade! For the first time in her life she had a semblance of independent freedom, and she didn't want to waste it by pining for a man who didn't even like her. Hell, he barely seemed to notice she existed.

This marriage wasn't about lust and need. It wasn't about him.

It was about *her*. It was her vehicle to going out into the world at last.

A whisper of discontent breezed through her but, as always, Emmeline ignored it. She had stayed at Annersty, stayed under the same roof as her father, because it had been the *right* thing to do. Just as marrying Pietro to assuage her father's obvious concerns was the *right* thing to do.

And the fact that it spoke of a lack of faith in her own abilities? That it spoke of her being infantilised to an unbearable degree? She wouldn't think about that. She *couldn't*. For she knew where that path would take her, and criticising her father, whom she adored, was not something she would countenance.

All that mattered was that she had left home— *finally*. She was in Rome. A smile tickled at her lips and once more she felt the sunshine warm her skin.

At twenty-two, she'd finally done it!

Her phone buzzed, startling her out of her reverie. She lifted it from the back pocket of her jeans and Pietro's face stared back at her from the screen.

Her heart pounded as she swiped the screen across. 'Hello?'

'Emmeline.'

There it was again. The warm butter oozing over her skin. She closed her eyes and sank to the ground so that she could give him the full force of her concentration.

'Are you there?'

'Oh.' She blinked her eyes open and nodded. 'Yes. What is it?'

'Your father is coming for dinner tonight. Seven o'clock.'

Silence prickled between them. Then, 'Daddy's coming...*here*?'

'*Certamente*. Naturally I presumed you'd want to see him again before he leaves for the States.'

Emmeline nodded, but consternation ran through her. She *had* intended to see her father again—only for coffee the following morning, when it could be just the two of them.

'Right.' She bit down on her lip.

'My assistant will let Signora Verdi know,' he said, referring to the housekeeper Emmeline had met once or twice. A matronly woman who filled her with a sense of awe.

'Fine,' she said, a little too sharply.

'Though he knows our marriage was arranged to serve a purpose, I think it would be good for him to see that we are...getting along.'

Emmeline's stomach churned. *But we're not*.

'Do you?' she asked.

'*Si*. He loves you very much,' Pietro said, but his tone was weary. Impatient. 'Seeing you happy will make *him* happy.'

'So you want me to fake it?' she snapped, before she could catch back the sarcastic rejoinder.

'I want you to think of your *father*,' he said softly. 'As you've proved yourself so very good at in the past.'

'What's that supposed to mean?'

'You married me to make him happy.'

A woman's voice filtered through into the call and acid spiked Emmeline's blood. She couldn't make out what the woman said, but the tone was low. *Personal*.

Jealousy—unmistakable—pricked at her flesh.

'I'll be home by six. And, Emmeline? Perhaps wear a dress.'

Outrage simmered in her blood as she disconnected the call. Wear a damned *dress*? He actually thought he could boss her into wearing whatever the hell *he* wanted? What *he* thought would be appropriate? True, since their wedding she'd gone back to the clothes she felt most comfortable in, and they were hardly the kind of clothes that would set the world on fire. But of all the rude, misogynistic, barbaric things to say!

She stood up, her hands shaking as she jammed the phone back in her pocket and stared out at Rome.

She'd show him, wouldn't she?

At ten minutes past six Emmeline walked into the formal dining room, intending to pour herself a stiff drink to steel her nerves. What she hadn't expected was to see her husband already at the bar, shaking a cocktail mixer.

She froze on the threshold, taking a deep breath. She had only a second to compose her face into a mask of calm before he looked up. And when their eyes met she was thrilled to bits that she'd put her plan into action.

It had involved hours of shopping—her least favourite activity by a mile—but the effect was worth it.

The dress was exquisite. It had the advantage of looking as though it had been made for her—in a silk fabric that clung to her breasts and hips and stopped several inches shy of her knee—and it had batwing sleeves that fell to halfway down her hands, giving her a sense of comfort. The front had a deep vee—far deeper than she'd worn in her life before. She'd teamed it with a pair of espadrilles, which made the look a little more casual for an at-home dinner.

'I'll have what you're having,' she murmured, with a veneer of confidence she was far from feeling.

He began to shake the drink once more with a tight nod. 'Nice dress.'

The compliment made heat flood through her body. 'Thanks.'

'It makes it almost impossible to remember that you're a sweet and innocent little virgin bride.'

Emmeline fought her natural reaction of embarrassment, which he must have been trying to goad her towards. She saw beyond it. Her eyes narrowed and she moved closer, watching as he poured the martini into a glass and curling her fingers around its stem before he could even offer it to her.

'That bothers you?'

'It confuses me,' he corrected, reaching for more bottles of alcohol and sloshing it into the mixer. 'Particularly when you are dressed like this.'

'So one's choice of attire is an indicator of sexual inclination?'

'No. But dressed like this you are…irresistible.'

She sipped her drink to hide her reaction, and then spluttered as the alcohol burned its way down her throat. 'Ugh—that's strong.'

'It's a martini,' he pointed out seriously. 'It's meant to be strong.'

She nodded, taking another sip, and this time it went down more easily.

'Why do you dress like you do?' He returned to their previous conversation.

'Why is it any of your business?' she fired back, her eyes holding his even when she wanted to look away.

'It interests me. You are an attractive woman who goes out of her way to hide her assets. It makes no sense.'

Emmeline turned away from him, surprised by how easily he'd surmised the truth of her situation. 'Not everyone thinks their worth is derived from their appeal to the opposite sex.'

He made a sound of disagreement. 'But to take pride in one's appearance isn't just about meeting someone, or attracting a lover. It's a sign of self-love to want to look your best.'

'I don't agree,' she murmured, even though she'd never really thought beyond the opinions she'd formed in her teenage years.

'But don't you feel *better* in this dress?'

He walked towards her, a glass in his hand, his eyes holding hers. She stared at him, refusing to cower even as nerves fluttered inside her.

'Don't you *like* the way you look tonight?'

'I don't like the way you're looking at me as though you want to rip it off,' she said thickly, sipping her drink.

His laugh was a slow, sensual cord, wrapping around her. And was she imagining there was something like tension in the harmless sound? The air in her lungs was burning, exploding...

'We've already discussed that. I'm not interested in being the man who teaches you to feel.'

He lifted a finger and ran it across her lower lip, then dragged it lower, and lower still, to the fabric that joined at the centre of her chest. Then lower to her navel. She gasped as he ran it over her womanhood and paused, lingering there, padding his thumb across a part of her body that no man had ever touched.

'Though I'd be lying if I said that right now it doesn't hold at least *some* appeal.' His words appeared to be almost dragged from him, as though against his will.

Confusion and doubt were back. Uncertainty. Her insides were swirling and without her knowledge her body swayed forward.

'I wonder if you would orgasm quickly…' he murmured distractedly, and a sharp swell of need made her groan.

She nodded—but what was she even nodding at?

His lips twisted into a hard-fought smile and he pulled his hand away. She made a small whimper of anger, and before she knew what she was doing her free hand had curled around his wrist, catching it and dragging him back.

'Careful, *cara*. I don't think you want to play with a man like me.'

'Why are you tormenting me, then?' she asked thickly, holding his hand still and pushing herself against him, her eyes wide, her body screaming with need. 'Why stir me up and then walk away? Is that *fun* for you? Do you *like* seeing me like this?'

'Fun? No. As for why I like doing this… I can't say. I suppose I'm a little like a cat with a ball of wool. The idea of a twenty-two-year-old virgin is not something I can understand. You fascinate me and I just don't seem able to help myself.'

'Then don't,' she whispered, sipping the last of her drink. 'Please.' She lifted her arms around his neck, and her lips sought his. *'Please.'*

'You're Col's daughter.' The words were gravelled. Dark and husky.

'And yet you married me.' She ground her hips against him, her eyes showing her every need and desire.

He swore into her mouth in his own language, and then his hand was running down her thigh, finding the hem of her dress and lifting it, pushing aside the fabric of her silky underwear. He brushed his fingers over her throbbing heat and she gasped, the sensation unlike anything she could have imagined.

'I'm not the right man for you to want,' he said.

And he was so right. But sensual need had overtaken any vestige of common sense.

'Shut up,' she said hungrily, and he laughed against her lips.

'Shut up and do this?' he asked, pushing aside the fabric of her underwear.

Her heart skidded to a stop. All she could do was wait. Wait for what came next.

If Emmeline had been capable of rational thought she might have cared a little more that they were in a room anyone could have walked into at any point. But she didn't. Fortunately her husband had his wits about him, and Pietro used his body to guide her back, so that she collided with a wall near enough to a corner to provide some cover.

His finger invaded her heat gently at first, nudging inside, preparing her slowly for the unfamiliar sensation. She whimpered as he pushed deeper, a cry catching in her throat as she throbbed around him, her muscles tensing and squeezing.

'God,' she groaned, grinding her hips, and he laughed

softly, moving his finger in a swirling motion while his thumb found the cluster of nerves at her entrance and teased it.

Her blood was boiling beneath her skin like liquid iron. She breathed out hungrily, the rasping sounds punctuating the silence of the room, and then she bit down on her lip as the sensations began to overflow, making her face blotchy with heat and sweat bead on her brow. She curled her fingers into his hair, holding him tight, and scrunched up her eyes.

The overload of feeling was something she hadn't prepared for. Waves of arousal and satisfaction ebbed through her, rocking her to the core. She stayed perfectly still, letting them pound against her nerve-endings, and then she tilted her head back, resting it against the wall as her breathing slowed to normal.

He eased his finger out of her wet, pulsing core, and she made a small sound of surprise at the unwelcome abandonment. When she opened her eyes he was staring down at her, his cheeks slashed with dark colour, his eyes silently assessing.

The world stopped spinning.

Everything stopped except her breathing and her awakening.

She lifted a hand, curled her fingers into his shirt, needing him for support. She held him while she caught her breath—in and out, in and out—and he watched her the whole time.

Finally, after long moments of silent, stretching heat, he spoke.

'You are far too sensual to have been uninterested in sex. Were you forbidden from dating?'

Her mind was still reeling from what had just happened. 'I need a minute…'

She bit down on her lip but couldn't stop the smile that spread across her face. She was beautiful at any time, really, but like this she was angelic.

'What the hell was *that*?'

His frown showed confusion. 'What?'

'I… I just… *Wow.*'

His groan was somehow scathing. 'Tell me you have at least *touched* yourself?'

Should she have? God, she supposed she *should* have had at least a passing curiosity in her own sexual development. Shame that she hadn't ever explored this side of herself made her flush to the roots of her hair.

'I…'

'What the hell happened to you?' he muttered. 'How can you have ignored these feelings? This desire?'

She swallowed, but the insulting tone of his voice was making her defensive. 'Not everyone sees sex as the be-all and end-all…'

'Yes, they do,' he disputed, a rough smile in his voice. 'At least anyone who's had really great sex does.' He shook his head. 'I wish I'd known this about you before agreeing to this damned marriage,' he said angrily. 'You *need* to have sex. And fast. But not with me.'

Her heart turned over in her chest. 'Why not with you?' she prompted.

His eyes flashed with rich frustration. 'I told you. Educating virgins isn't my thing. I'm not looking for the complications of that.'

'Even with your *wife*?' she responded archly.

'Not a *real* wife, remember?'

She bit down on her lip and nodded. 'So? What am I meant to do?'

'Well, you've waited twenty-two years. I guess a few more won't kill you.'

But it might kill *him*, Pietro thought as he turned his back on her. Walking away as though he was completely unaffected was damned near impossible with the raging hard-on between his legs.

A virgin. And yet so gorgeous and wanton and sensual. God, he wanted to take her to his bed. Despite what he'd said, the idea of teaching Emmeline Morelli *just* what her body was capable of stirred all kinds of animalistic masculine fantasies in his mind.

Being the first man to move inside her… Hell, the need to possess her was so savage it was beneath him.

He couldn't do it.

He'd married her because he loved Col Bovington like a father, and he would resist the urge to sleep with Emmeline for that exact reason.

No matter how damned much he was tempted.

He was the adult. The *experienced* adult. He had to control this beast of desire that was burning between them or he'd never forgive himself.

'I've always liked Rome.'

Col's voice had a wistful note. Or maybe Pietro was imagining things, because, in the back of his mind—much as it must be in Col's—was one single question: was this the last time Col would come to Italy? Was this the last time he'd look down on this ancient city?

'It's a city like no other.' Pride pierced Pietro's statement.

'Si,' Col agreed, a smile on his face. His eyes scanned

the skyline, taking in the glistening lights of the city in the distance set against the inky black sky. 'How is she?'

Guilt slashed through Col. A feeling that was as unwelcome as it was foreign.

'Is she settling in? Happy? Adjusting?'

Pietro could close his eyes and remember the way her body had felt. The way her body had closed around his finger. The sounds she'd made as she'd come—hard.

He clamped his teeth together and focussed on the cupola of *il Vaticano*, willing his libido to remember where he was and with whom.

'It's still very early,' he said noncommittally.

'But you *are* getting along?' Col pushed.

Pietro expelled a breath. 'Sure.'

If you could count barely seeing each other and then him making her come for no reason other than he'd wanted to the second he'd seen her.

'Good.' If Col had doubts he didn't express them.

Pietro propped an elbow on the bannister and turned to face his friend slowly, weighing his words with caution. 'I think you need to tell her the truth.'

'About what?' Col joked.

It fell flat.

'She's stronger than you think.' God, Pietro hoped that was true. 'She'll cope with it. What she *won't* cope with is discovering you've lied to her.'

'I know her better than anyone.'

Col's words held a warning and Pietro heeded it. Not because he was afraid, but because the older man was probably right. Col had drawn a line in the sand and Pietro had no intention of walking over it.

He sighed gruffly. 'Then *consider* talking to her.'

'I can't. I need her to have more in her life than me.'

His eyes shifted to Pietro and his skin looked pale all over. 'If she knows she'll come home.'

'So? Let her.'

'No. *Damn it!* The whole point of this is... I don't want her to nurse me. She deserves better than that.'

Pietro was very still, watchful. Waiting. 'You don't want her to nurse you? She's your daughter. When my father was sick—'

'It's not the same.' Col seemed to wince at the abruptness of his answer. 'I'm sorry, Pietro. I don't mean to belittle what you went through. But it's not the same.'

'Why not?'

'Because she is my only child. She will be orphaned when I die. Because she adores me and idolises me and I will not have her seeing me weakened and bedridden.' His jaw clenched firmly. 'I love her too much for that.'

An aeroplane passed overhead, leaving a trail of white cloud shimmering against the night sky. Pietro stared at it for a moment, wondering about the plane's destination and the people that occupied its belly. He wondered too at Col's 'love'. *Was* it love that could so easily lie? *Could* you love someone and deny them an opportunity to say goodbye?

'Did you think he looked tired?' Emmeline asked when Pietro returned to the lounge room, having said farewell to the American Senator.

The question caught him off-guard in its directness and perception. Then again, she was the much-adored daughter of the man—of course she'd notice small changes.

'Perhaps.' He sidestepped the question with surprising difficulty, his gaze resting on Emmeline's face.

She was distracted, toying with the hem of her dress, her fingers running over its silky edge as she nodded slowly. He knew what that dress felt like because he'd held it in his hands. He'd touched it and run his fingers over it and then he'd found her heart and driven her crazy against the wall.

'He did. I suppose it's jetlag... Or something.' She shook her head. 'I don't know.'

He sucked himself back into the conversation with difficulty, his arousal straining against the fabric of his pants. It was unwanted. So was the guilt that was sledging through him. Guilt at deceiving her despite the fact he owed his loyalty to Col and not to Emmeline.

'I'm going out,' he murmured, speaking the words before he'd even realised what he'd intended.

'Out?' She frowned, flicking a glance to the slim wristwatch she wore. 'It's after ten.'

His laugh was softly mocking. 'In Roma that is still early, *cara.*'

Her cheeks darkened, and her eyes were huge in her face as she looked at him. Her pretty face twisted into an expression he didn't recognise, but then it was gone. She was herself again. Unfazed, uninterested.

'Fine,' she said. 'Thank you for tonight.'

'You're *thanking* me?' he said with disbelief. 'I invited your father here for my own purposes as much as yours.'

Her smile was a twist of pale pink lips and then she stood, moving towards him.

'I didn't mean for that.'

As she passed him he caught a hint of her vanilla and rosebud fragrance and his gut clenched with barely controlled need. The desire to snake his hand out and catch her around the waist, to pull her to him and make her come again, filled him like an explosion. His head turned as she left the room, following her by instinct. The way that dress pulled against the curves of her arse as she walked…the way her long legs glided as if she was in a damned ballet…

He needed to get out of the house before he did something really rash. Like give in to temptation and invite his wife to his bed…

CHAPTER FIVE

HIS BEDROOM WAS far enough away from hers that she wouldn't necessarily hear when he came home each night. But somehow in the month they'd been married her ears had trained themselves to hear the slightest noise.

Like the opening of his bedroom door and the shutting of it a second later.

She heard the tell-tale click and her eyes drifted to the bedside table. She reached for her phone, checking the time. It was just after two.

How did he do that so often and still look so damned fresh the next day?

She tried not to think about who he'd been with and where. Though she didn't need to be a genius to work it out.

He'd made no effort to hide his virility, and they'd agreed before marrying that he'd continue his life as before. And he was doing that. It was Emmeline's fault that it no longer sat well with her.

She turned over in the bed, flipping on to her other side so she could stare out of the window. It was still warm, with the breeze that drifted in offering a hint of relief—but not much. The day had been sticky.

Was there only one woman in his life? Was it the beautiful redhead from the wedding?

She closed her eyes and the woman's face came to mind. She'd been stunning—but so clearly cosmetically enhanced she should have borne her surgeon's signature somewhere on her body. Was that the kind of woman he went for?

Emmeline would never be like that.

She blinked her eyes open but it was too late. An image of her mother had seared into her brain and she made a small sound in the dark room.

Patrice Bovington had been beautiful too. Stunning without cosmetic enhancement. But that hadn't stopped her from seeing her doctor regularly, having a little Botox dabbed into her forehead, a tad of filler in her lips. Over the years she'd changed, but so subtly that it was only in looking back at photos that Emmeline could recognise the fact that beautifying herself had become an unhealthy obsession for her mother.

And a foolish one too. For there would always someone more beautiful, more svelte, younger. Why make one's appearance the hallmark of one's self-esteem?

'You could almost be pretty if you put some effort in.'

She sat upright in the bed, the fever in her blood burning out of control. Did he *know* that looking pretty had led to all the problems she'd had with her mother? Guilt made her stomach flop as she remembered their last argument. The day before Patrice had driven her Mercedes convertible into an enormous elm around the corner from the house.

Emmeline rolled back to her other side, staring at the wall now. But it was no good. Her mind was wide awake, her legs restless, her body warm.

She sat up, then pushed her feet out of the bed.

She'd only swum a handful of times since arriving at the villa. Both times when she'd known Pietro was out of the house.

And now he was fast asleep—probably exhausted from seducing some beautiful woman all evening.

Emmeline changed into her swimsuit quietly. If she could hear the sound of *his* door clicking open and shut then he could certainly hear hers. She tiptoed out into the corridor, pausing for a second, her breath offensively loud in the silent evening.

The stairs were around ten steps away. She moved quietly but quickly, like some kind of night-time ninja.

She'd just wrapped her fingers around the top of the bannister when his door was flung open.

He stood there in a pair of shorts, otherwise naked, his scowl landing on her as though she'd driven a herd of elephants through the house.

'Did I wake you?' she whispered, not sure why she was keeping her voice down given the fact they were the only two in the house.

'No. I was up.' His eyes dropped to the swimsuit that was clearly on display, his frown deepening. 'It appears we've had the same idea.'

'Oh.' She didn't dare look at his shorts but, yes, she supposed they *could* be swimming trunks. 'It's a hot night...' she finished lamely.

His grunt was an agreement of sorts.

She prevaricated on the steps for a moment, contemplating going back to her room and then deciding against it. When he began to move towards her, though, her pulse kicked up a notch. Her breath was held in her throat.

'What are you doing?'

He looked at her as though she'd gone mad. 'Going for a swim. We just discussed this.'

'Oh. I thought…' She closed her eyes and breathed in deeply; it was a mistake. The smell of him filled her, reminding her of how it had felt when he'd touched her so intimately.

'The pool is more than big enough for the both of us.'

He was right, of course, and now she felt like an even bigger idiot. It was bad enough that he thought her some kind of inexperienced prim virgin. Worse when she confirmed those thoughts by acting just like one.

'I know that,' she snapped, resuming her journey down the stairs, moving quickly to stay ahead of him.

At the bottom she moved ahead—not waiting for him, not wanting him to think that she saw this as a joint venture. He wanted to swim and she wanted to swim. That didn't mean they would be swimming *together*.

The air on the deck was noticeably cooler, but it was still a sultry, muggy night. It felt as though a huge bandage was pressing down on Rome, holding in its heat, making breathing difficult.

Emmeline dropped her towel onto a lounger and turned towards the pool—just as Pietro dived into the water, his body strong and flexed as he hit the surface and went underneath.

He was like a god, tanned and muscular, as if he'd been carved from stone. She watched the water separate as if to welcome him and then conceal him again, almost by magic. Her breath was held again inside her lungs—waiting, apparently, for the moment he reappeared at the other end of the pool when she let out a slow sigh.

'Well?' He turned to face her. 'Are you joining me, Mrs Morelli?'

Her eyes met his, and if she'd known about the look of anguished surrender in them she would have tried harder to conceal her feelings. But she didn't.

The moonlight sliced through her as she moved to the water's edge and dipped her toe in. As she'd hoped, it was deliciously cool.

She sat on the edge and then eased herself into the water. It reached up to her waist and enveloped her in its thick, luxuriant relief.

She didn't swim. Rather she walked across the pool, her face deliberately averted from his. He might have found it entertaining if he hadn't already been frustrated beyond belief. The idea of a cold swim had been essentially to serve the same purpose a cold shower might have. Instead his wife was swimming with him, her pert breasts outlined by the light cast from the moon, her enigmatic, aristocratic face tilted angrily away from him.

Was she angry with him? And, if so, why did he like the idea so much? Why did he want to inspire that hot, fierce temper in her?

He dived underwater and swam the length of the pool, pretending not to notice as he passed her by and splashed water in her general direction.

When he surfaced she'd moved to the other end of the pool.

Was she hiding from him? The idea of her being the mouse to his cat was like a red rag to a bull. He dived underwater again and swam beneath the surface, stealthy and silent, and had the pleasure of seeing surprise on her face when he lifted himself up right beside her.

'Nice evening?' she murmured, her eyes scanning his face, her anger flashing more visibly now.

'Not really,' he said noncommittally.

Without developing some kind of mystical psychic ability she had no idea what he meant by that. She turned her head away, her eyes soaking in the view of Rome in the distance without really seeing it. Even at this early hour of the morning the city was alive, its buildings outlined with light, all its ancient stories winding around themselves, whispering through the walls to those who wanted to listen.

'Do you do this often?' He turned to face her, his body achingly close.

'No.'

'Nor do I. Strange that we both had the same idea tonight.'

'Not really. It's been muggy as hell today,' she pointed out logically. 'I couldn't sleep.'

He nodded, but his eyes were speculative. 'And in general?' he prompted.

God, she looked young like this—bathed in moonlight and the salt water of his pool.

Her eyes were blank. 'What do you mean?'

He compressed his lips. 'Are you settling in well to Rome?'

'Oh.' She was grateful for the night, grateful that it hid her blush. 'Yes. I've sent off my enrolment forms. I'll start university next term.'

'What will you study?'

'Psychology.' She looked away from his intense gaze,

feeling that he saw way too much. 'It's always interested me.'

'I see.' He frowned thoughtfully. 'I would have imagined you doing history, or perhaps English literature.'

She lifted a hand and ran it over the water's surface, feeling its thick undulations beneath her fingertips.

'Why? Because I'm bookish? Because I look as though I'd be perfectly at home under bags of dust in an ancient library?'

His smile was perfunctory. 'No.'

He moved closer towards her, and again she had the sense that he was chasing her. Ridiculous when they were simply floating at the same end of the pool. Besides, why would a man like Pietro Morelli chase her?

'Because the last time I saw you, you spent the entire night staring at very old paintings as though they were the beginning and end of your existence.'

Emmeline's smile was genuine. 'I'd never seen works of art like that before. The Dutch Masters have always fascinated me.'

'So you can see, then, why I thought of history—perhaps art history—as your university subject of choice?'

'Oh, I *love* art.' She nodded. 'And old things in general.' She tilted her head back into the water, wetting her hair. It draped down her back like a silken curtain. 'But I've wanted to do psychology for almost as long as I can remember.'

Not quite true. She could recall the exact moment when it had dawned on her that a lot of people's minds needed fixing.

Apparently Pietro was drawing the same conclusion. 'When did you learn the truth about your mother's death?'

'I thought I told you?' she murmured quietly, feeling the night wrapping around them like a blanket. 'I knew at the time.'

'I'm sorry you had to experience that loss. And so young.'

Emmeline rarely spoke about her mother. Her father never wanted to talk about her, and Emmeline didn't really have anyone else to confide in about something of that nature. But, perhaps because Pietro had known Patrice, Emmeline felt her strongly held borders dropping.

'She'd been unhappy for a long time. I didn't expect her to die, but it wasn't a complete surprise, somehow.'

'Unhappy how?' Pietro pushed, moving closer.

His recollections of Patrice were vague. She'd been drop-dead gorgeous, and kind enough. Perhaps there'd been a coldness to her, a sense of disconnection. He'd been a young man when he'd last seen her and his thoughts weren't easy to recall.

'Oh, you know…' Emmeline's smile was uneven, her eyes not quite meeting his.

'No, I don't. That's why I asked you.'

How could Emmeline answer? There'd been that morning when she'd come downstairs to find her mother passed out, two empty bottles of gin at her feet, her make-up ruined by her tears. And there'd been all the little nips and tucks, of course. But the biggest clue had been the control she'd begun to exert over Emmeline.

Even as a teenager Emmeline had known it wasn't right—that there was something unhealthy about her mother's desire to infantilise Emmeline, to keep her from experimenting with clothes and fashion. Discouraging Emmeline's attempts on improving her image had been one thing, but knowingly pushing her towards un-flattering hairstyles and prohibiting her from anything except the wardrobe she, Patrice, had selected…

It had taken years for Emmeline to understand her mother's motivations and they'd left her reeling.

'Lots of things,' she said vaguely, shaking her head.

Perhaps it was the raw pain in his wife's voice that stalled Pietro from pushing further. For whatever reason, he let the matter go for a moment.

'Psychology will no doubt be very interesting,' he said quietly. 'When do you begin?'

'A month.'

He nodded. 'There's still time for you to adapt to life here, then.'

'I think I'm just about adapted,' she said quietly.

He was so close now that when he moved the water rippled in response and it almost felt as though he was touching her. She knew she should put some distance between them, but she'd hardly seen him for a month. This nearness was like a highly addictive form of crack cocaine.

'You have been bunkered here in the villa,' he said softly. 'It's time for you to start coming out with me. You are my wife. There are events. Functions. Things to attend.'

'Oh.' She bit down on her lip and uncertainty glimmered in her eyes. She had been the one who'd suggested they needed to keep up a certain public persona. But now the idea filled her with doubts. 'I don't know if that's really necessary…'

'Not all the time, no. But there are certain things you can no longer avoid.'

'I haven't been *avoiding* anything.'

As soon as she said it she knew it was a lie. She *had* been holed up in his house as much as possible—reading, emailing, reading some more. Keeping her ears permanently trained on noises that might herald Pietro's arrival so that she could scamper away.

'My bank organises a banquet every summer. It is a Midsummer's Eve theme—very beautiful and enjoyable. You'll come with me.'

She arched a brow, instantly resenting his imperious tone. 'Oh, I will, will I?'

'Si.'

His fingers brushed against hers underwater. Surely it wasn't an accident? Her heart didn't think it was. It pounded hard against the fabric of her being with a thundering beat that he must be able to hear.

'I usually take a date. That would raise eyebrows this year.'

She smiled, but it was a distracted smile. He'd been late home almost every night in the month since they had been married. It was impossible to believe he hadn't been seen out with different women in that time.

The thought made her heart race, but for a less palatable reason now. *Jealousy.* Not because she cared for him or wanted him, she hastened to reassure herself. But because he was *hers.* Her husband. And she didn't particularly want people thinking that he was straying from the marital bed already.

Marital bed.

What a joke.

Longing surged inside her.

The need he had awoken was at fever-pitch.

She controlled it as best she could, but her mind continued to toss up images of just what it would be like to be made love to by a man like her husband.

The reality wouldn't live up to her fantasies, Emmeline was certain.

'It's Friday night,' he murmured.

Her eyes clashed with his and the longing was back, begging her to do something—anything—to indulge it.

'You want me to go?' she asked quietly.

'I think you should come, *si*.'

She bit down on her lip, and then spoke before she could question the wisdom of her proposition.

'Well,' she said thoughtfully, 'there's something I want too. I suggest we…trade.'

'Oh? And what is it that you want, Mrs Morelli?'

Say the words… Say the words… her courage pushed angrily.

'I want you to sleep with me.'

They blurted out of her on the warm breeze that rushed past.

Pietro barely reacted. Just a tightening around his lips showed that he'd heard her proposition and was digesting it.

'I told you—'

Emmeline waved a hand in the air. 'That you're not interested in being my first lover,' she said, with a shrug of her shoulders. 'But it's too late for that. You've shown me what my body can feel and I want to know more.'

'I'm not a damned *teacher*.'

'No. You're my husband.'

His eyes narrowed, and his breath was clearly tearing from his body.

'I'm not going to sleep with you,' he said with an angry shake of his head.

God, she was Col's *daughter*, and he'd married her to ease the mind of his dying friend.

But surely Col knew enough of Pietro's ways to know that this was a possibility.

Why was Pietro fighting it so hard?

The last month had been a living torture as he'd forced himself to keep his distance, never sure if the flame between them would burst out of control.

'I'll go to this…this banquet with you. And whatever else you want me to attend. But I need to know what it feels like.'

'Why now?' he asked, the question thick in his throat.

'I didn't *mean* to not sleep with anyone. I just never met a guy I was interested in. Honestly, I started to think I was kind of…sexually not all *there*. All my friends have been in relationships forever.' She bit down on her lip.

'You lost your mother at a vulnerable time in your life,' he said gently.

'Yes, that's true. It changed who I am.' Her clear amber gaze held his for a long moment. 'Life sort of got away from me. I feel like I've spent the last seven years in a sort of stasis and now I'm ready to start living again. I want to wake up.'

Be brave. Be brave.

She closed the distance between them, surprising him when she wrapped her arms around his neck. 'I want *you* to wake me up.'

His eyes were lightly mocking as they stared back down at her, but he didn't push her away. He didn't remove her touch.

'I'm not Prince Charming, Sleeping Beauty.' The words were cold. Determined.

'I know that.' She blinked her eyes. 'I don't need you to be.'

'I wouldn't have married you if I'd known,' he said with an angry shake of his head. 'You deserve to find someone yourself. Someone you care about.'

'She'll be vulnerable to fortune-hunters.'

Yes, Emmeline—the sweet, naïve virgin heiress— sure as hell would have been vulnerable. She might as well have had a target on her back for some guy to come along and sweep her off her feet.

All Col's reasons for pursuing this marriage were blindingly clear to Pietro. What had at one point seemed ridiculously absurd now made absolute sense. Even without the fortune she would inherit, her youthful innocence would mark her as the easiest target for no-good bastards on the lookout for an easy buck.

'This isn't about happily-ever-after,' Emmeline said with a grim determination. 'I'm twenty-two, and until our wedding day I'd never even kissed a guy.'

She dropped her eyes, the admission making her insides squirm with embarrassment.

'I feel like some dusty old antique no one's wanted to pick up off the shelf.' Her throat moved as she swallowed. 'But when you look at me it's like... I *get* it. I get what everyone's talking about. I understand—finally— the appeal of sex. And I don't want to die a virgin.'

He couldn't help but laugh softly at her dramatic end note. 'You are not going to die a virgin. You are still young.'

'Yes, but...if not now, when? *Who?*'

An excellent question.

Suddenly the idea of someone else taking this precious gift was anathema to Pietro. The red-blooded man that was thick in his blood had begun to see his wife as *his*. Not just a bride of convenience, but a woman in *his* home, under *his* protection. Was he to let her go one day, knowing some other man would take what he, Pietro, had so nobly declined?

He groaned softly, knowing then that the devil was on his shoulder and he was listening to his urgings. He was listening when he should be speaking sense, reminding her of what they were.

'You are too young for me,' he said, with a finality that his hard-as-stone cock wasn't happy with. 'And too inexperienced.'

He reached up, wrapping his hands around her wrists, pulling them away from his neck. As he glided them through the water, resting them at her sides, her pert breasts pressed into him.

His arousal jerked and for the briefest moment his will-power left him. How easy it would be to do what she wanted! She was handing herself to him on a silver platter.

But he'd regret it.

One way or another he'd conquer this desire—because nothing and no one *ever* got the best of Pietro Morelli.

CHAPTER SIX

DIO. SINCE WHEN had she started wearing skirts like that?

Pietro stared out of the villa window, his concentration sapped by the image of his wife in a scrap of denim that barely covered her arse and a simple white strappy top.

Without a bra.

The pert outlines of her breasts were clearly visible, as were the hardened nubs of her nipples, straining at the fabric. She was tapping a pen against her mouth, her eyes intent on the book she had propped on her knees. But his eyes were lost on her lips. Lips that were slightly parted, full and pink, glistening as though she'd just licked them.

'I'm twenty-two and until our wedding day I'd never kissed a guy.'

A fierce burst of possession tore through him. Those lips had welcomed his claim on them, had sought his mouth and kissed him back. They'd parted for his invasion.

She'd tasted so sweet.

His eyes swept closed as he remembered the way she'd come to him on their wedding night, all pink-cheeked and nervous. The way she'd stood like a rabbit caught in bright headlights—which was exactly what she'd been! How could she have understood the onslaught of sensual heat that was flaring up between them?

Even for Pietro it was proving difficult to process. And impossible to ignore, apparently. Did she have any idea what her presence was doing to him? Here in his house...his virgin bride?

His for the taking.

The idea spread like wildfire through his body. It took every ounce of his willpower not to give in to temptation and act on it.

But it would be so wrong. Other women were for meaningless sex. She was *different*. Not someone he could desire. She was someone he needed to protect. Yes, as a brother would protect his sister.

Ugh. Not as a brother!

She tossed her dark hair over one shoulder and her eyes lifted almost unconsciously. She was clearly lost in thought, her mind wandering as her eyes did the same.

Pietro jerked his own head down, returning his concentration to the marketing reports he'd been given that morning. Or at least pretending to.

But it was incredibly dull reading, and his wife was just metres away, her long legs calling to him...

With a noise of impatience he scraped his chair back and strode towards the glass doors, his expression grim.

'Are you wearing suntan lotion?' he asked, pushing the door open wider as he stepped through it.

Emmeline's frown showed that she'd been deep in thought—that his question had seemed to come from a long way away.

'Are you wearing suntan lotion?'

Her face showed bemusement. 'No. But it's after five. I'm sure I'll be—'

'The Roman sun still has bite.' He turned on his heel and disappeared, returning a moment later with a small yellow tube. 'Here.'

He tossed it down on the lounger and she picked it up, unscrewing the lid slowly. His eyes followed her progress and he crossed his arms over his chest, his manner imposing.

He had been imposing even *before* Emmeline had factored in her embarrassing confession and request in the pool last night. No. Not last night: in the early hours of that same morning.

The colour in her cheeks now had nothing to do with the fact that she'd been reading by the pool for hours. Though why she'd chosen to return to the scene of the crime was beyond Emmeline. In that moment, confronted by the ghost of what a fool she'd been, she wished she was anywhere else.

She flicked the cap off the bottle and squeezed some cream into her hands, then rubbed it over her exposed arms and the vee of her neck.

Pietro watched, but his temper wasn't improved by the display. Nor was it improved when she placed more cream into her palm and reached down to spread it over her legs. Legs that were long, tanned and smooth...

He looked away from her, his arms still crossed.

But he could see her in his mind. As she'd been in the pool early that morning—her hair like a shimmering black veil, her eyes enormous, her lips curved into a smile.

Her question hadn't been unreasonable. Hell, he'd

backed her up against a wall and slid a finger into her wet heat until she'd come in his arms. Of *course* she was curious.

He'd stirred something inside her and now he was preventing her from experimenting. From exploring that side of her.

It wasn't fair.

Was she annoyed that he'd turned her down?

'The thing is,' he said, as though their conversation from the night before was still going, had simply been paused for a few hours while they slept and he worked. 'You're my wife, and if we were to sleep together it would be too complicated…'

Her eyes flew to his face, the statement knocking her off balance completely. She hadn't expected this, but she managed to pick up the threads of their negotiation as though it were just that—a simple business deal.

'Complicated how?'

'I have nothing to offer.' He spoke stiffly, his shoulders squared. 'I'm not interested in a relationship, and I suspect you'll blur those lines if I do what you ask of me.'

She nodded slowly and then shrugged her shoulders. 'Sure.'

Her easy acceptance was insulting. 'If you came to want more from me I can promise you I wouldn't offer it.'

She bit down on her lip and shrugged once more. 'Whatever. It's not important. Forget I mentioned it.'

He looked away once more. *Why* did she have such beautiful legs? Out of nowhere he pictured them wrapped around his waist as he pulled her closer, pressing into her.

His arousal throbbed painfully.

'I know I can't hold a candle to your usual…um… lovers. It was stupid of me to even suggest it.'

'You are *very* different,' he agreed softly.

Her battered pride was almost debilitating in its intensity. He didn't need to *tell* her how different she was. She'd seen the photos. He'd all but told her that she wasn't attractive. God, she'd thrown herself at his feet! Of all the foolish, embarrassing, childish, stupid things to do!

Regret washed over her heart. But pride was beating its drum, forcing her to remember who she was and what she wanted in life. This marriage was a stepping stone for Emmeline—a brick path to freedom.

'I think I just got carried away last night. The moon… The water… The heat…' Her smile was dismissive. 'It won't happen again.'

She briefly met his eyes and then looked back to her book, pretending fascination with the page she was on even as the words swam before her eyes.

It won't happen again.

'That is for the best, *cara*.'

He spun on his heel and stalked back inside the villa before he gave in to temptation and pulled her to her feet, roughly against his chest, and plundered those sweet lips that had been tempting him all afternoon.

Rafe let out a low whistle, his eyes locked on some point across the room. Pietro followed his brother's gaze, though he knew what he'd see.

His wife, Emmeline Morelli, looking as if she'd walked out of a goddamned *Vogue* photo-shoot. Her dress was beautiful, but every woman at this event was draped in couture and dripping with diamonds. It was Emmeline he saw.

Her long dark hair had been set in loose curls that waved around her back, and the dress itself was a sort of Grecian style, in a cream fabric that gathered beneath her breasts then fell in floaty, gauzy swathes to her feet, which were clad in shimmering gold sandals. She wore a snake bracelet on her upper arm, and a circle of gold around her head.

She looked like a very beautiful, very sexy fairy. Something the two men she had been locked in conversation with for the past twenty minutes seemed eminently aware of. Her face was animated as they spoke, her eyes illuminated and her laugh frequent.

Hot, white need snaked through him.

'Married life seems to agree with Mrs Morelli,' Rafe said, and grinned, grabbing a glass of wine from a tray being walked past by a waiter.

'*Si,*' Pietro agreed, willing himself to look away but finding it almost impossible.

'And you?' Rafe turned to study his brother, a smile twitching at the corners of his lips. 'I would ask how *you're* finding the leap into married life, but I can see for myself that it is no hardship.'

Pietro's expression was shuttered.

'No comment, eh?' Rafe laughed good-naturedly.

A muscle jerked in Pietro's jaw. 'There are too many of these twinkling lights,' he snapped, changing the subject. 'I feel like they are everywhere I look.'

Rafe's laugh was annoying Pietro. *Everything* was annoying him. Who the hell *were* those men? Had she met them before? It was possible that they had dealings in America…that they knew Col. Perhaps she'd hosted them at the plantation. Maybe they were old friends.

A groan of resentment died in his throat. He nodded dismissively at his brother. 'I'll speak to you later.'

Pietro moved quickly, cutting through the crowd, ignoring any attempt to draw him into conversation. But there were so many people between him and his wife and he was the man of the hour, in huge demand.

He spent a few minutes in curt exchange with a board member, and then smiled briefly at his cousin Lorena before getting within striking range of his wife.

He paused, watching her up close for a few seconds, seeing the way her face moved while in conversation.

Guilt was not something he was used to and yet he felt it now. Her father was one of his most valued friends, and yet he'd hardly taken the time to speak to Emmeline. What was making her laugh like that? What did she find funny?

He compressed his lips and moved closer, but at the moment of his approach the two men stepped away— not before one of them pressed a kiss against Emmeline's cheek and almost earned an angry rebuke from Pietro.

'Oh, Pietro.' She blinked up at him, her expression shifting swiftly from enthusiasm to confusion.

His chest felt as if it had been rolled over by a car. He manoeuvred his body, placing himself between Emmeline and the crowd, her back almost touching the wall, so that both of them would be reminded of the night he'd made her come.

Her breath snagged in her throat. She stared up at him, a pulse beating wildly in her throat.

'Who were those men?'

A frown tugged at her lips, but only for a second. Then the enthusiasm was back in her eyes, apparently irrepressible.

'Oh, they're professors at the university! One of them is a lecturer in the psychology department. It's going to be so helpful to have people there I know already.'

Great. She'd continue to see people who looked at her as though she was an ice cream they wanted to lick regularly.

Anger made common sense impossible. 'You should be with me,' he grunted angrily. 'Not talking to strange men.'

'They weren't *strange* men—they were perfectly nice. And staying with you at something like this is impossible,' she responded curtly. 'Everyone wants to talk to *you*, not me.'

'I don't care; you're my wife.'

'Yes, your *wife*. Not an accessory,' she pointed out softly, keeping her voice low purely out of recognition of the fact that there were people everywhere.

'We agreed that we wouldn't draw attention to our relationship or lack thereof. I will *not* have people gossip that my wife's interest is straying.'

She blinked up at him, her face pale. 'You must be kidding me! Your ego is wounded because I was talking to two probably married professors from the university I'm going to attend?'

'You weren't just *talking*. You were...'

'What? You think I was *flirting*?' she said with disbelief. 'You're unbelievable.'

'Forse,' he acknowledged. 'Nevertheless, I want you to stay with me tonight.'

Emmeline glared up at him angrily. She might have

moved hell and high water to please her father, but that was where her submissive tendencies ended.

'No way.' To her chagrin, tears sparkled on her eyelashes. She blinked them away angrily. 'Right now you're the last person I want to see.'

And then, with her back up against the wall—literally—he placed a hand on her hip and stroked her flesh gently, teasing her, making her pulse throb.

'Why do I find that so hard to believe?' he asked throatily, the words a hoarse demand.

'Don't.'

She bit down on her lower lip, and there was such a look of need in her eyes and confusion in her face that he almost dropped his hand.

Almost...but not quite. 'Don't what?'

Don't use this against me, she thought, her heart hurting. This desire she wasn't used to was tormenting her enough already.

He moved a little closer, dropping his head by degrees, so that when he spoke his words were whispered into her ear. 'Go and wait for me in the car. It's time for us to leave.'

'We've only been here an hour,' she pointed out huskily, her body attuned to every shift in his.

'Fifty-nine minutes too long,' he responded.

'Why are we leaving?'

Because I don't want to watch you being drooled over by any other man.

Because I want to make love to you.

Because you're mine.

He shook his head. 'It's time. I'll be out as soon as possible.'

But it was not so easy for Pietro to depart. By the

time he'd said goodbye to the more influential of the guests Emmeline had been cooling her heels in the car for almost a half-hour, and it was clear that she was in a foul mood.

'Am I being punished for enjoying a conversation?' she demanded, the second he was in the driver's seat.

'No.' He revved the car to life and floored the accelerator.

He shifted a sidelong look her way. Her jaw was clenched, her hands gripped tightly in her lap, her body vibrating with barely suppressed anger.

'I went to a lot of effort to come to this damned thing tonight because you told me you wanted me to! No, you told me I *had* to! I don't appreciate being frog-marched out like some errant schoolgirl.'

Oh, God. The last thing he needed was to picture his wife as a schoolgirl. *Hell.* She *had* been a schoolgirl the first time he'd seen her, around the time of Patrice's funeral. She'd appeared in the hallway in a navy blue dress, with a blazer that fell to her hips, and even then Pietro had known she had the potential to be trouble for him.

He had unconsciously stayed away from the plantation after that, avoiding her as much as he could. It hadn't always been possible—there'd been a few dinners and parties, in the intervening years—but for the most part he'd kept a very wise distance.

Something about Col Bovington's daughter had sent all his warning sensors haywire, and now he knew how right his instincts had been.

'I was having a good time,' she continued angrily, her gaze focussed on the streets of Rome as they drove.

She didn't know it well enough yet to recognise that they were heading out of the city—away from his villa.

'I'm glad,' he said quietly. 'But those men were all over you and you were encouraging them.'

'How can you *say* that? We were just talking.'

'Believe me, *cara*, with you in that dress no man will be "just talking" to you.'

Her jaw dropped and she whipped around to face him, her face lashed by pain. 'It's a *nice* dress. A *respectable* dress.'

'You look good enough to eat—and I'm sure as hell not the only man who thought so.'

Emmeline's face drained of all colour, and all the fight seemed to leave her in one second.

Pietro didn't notice.

'You're my *wife*! It doesn't matter that our marriage is unconventional. I will not have you dragging my name through the mud…'

'Your name…' She rolled her eyes, but her words were just a whisper. 'For such a powerful, successful guy, you've got major insecurity about your reputation.'

He slammed his palm into the steering wheel, anger coursing through him. It wasn't about that! Didn't she understand? He had *no* insecurities; his virility left him little room for doubt on that score. It was just a stupid excuse. Something he could say that would achieve the desired result—which was what? Her total isolation? *Dio.* What kind of barbaric son-of-a-bitch was he turning into?

'*You* said I should change how I look.'

She was shivering now—a reaction Pietro finally recognised, though he couldn't understand it. Unconsciously he drove faster, turning the car onto the high-way and picking up speed.

'You said that I had to be what people would expect of your wife. Haven't I done that?'

He gripped the steering wheel tighter, his eyes focussed on the night sky ahead. She'd done it—only far too well for his liking.

'You would have complained if I'd come to that thing tonight wearing something I was comfortable in—something I usually wear. Now you're complaining because I'm dressed like any of those other women who were there.' She shook her head from side to side. 'That's not fair.'

It wasn't—she was right. But nothing about this was fair! He'd been *happy* before marrying Emme-line. Happy in his life…happy with the endless parade of women he'd taken to his bed.

And now?

He had no damned idea.

'Where are we going?' she asked, as if waking from a dream and suddenly realising that they were well outside the city.

'Not much further,' he promised, his eyes flicking to the clock in the centre of the dashboard, willing the distance to shorten. 'Close your eyes, *cara*.'

'I'm too angry to sleep,' she snapped, but she did sit back in her seat, and a moment later her eyes fluttered closed.

Her steady, rhythmic breathing informed him that she'd drifted off despite her protestations. He drove the rest of the way in a silent car, but his thoughts were still screaming at him.

What he was planning was stupid, crazy, and he'd

decided firmly against it. But after seeing her with those men… He no longer had a choice.

He pulled the car through the electric gates to the farmhouse and then crept up the gravelled driveway.

Though no one lived there, he had a team who kept it permanently tidy and stocked.

His headlights illuminated the pots of geraniums and lavender that stood on either side of the green-painted door.

He went inside, checking from room to room, leaving the bedroom until last. It was an enormous space, with an old iron bed in the middle. The floor was tiled and the shutters were closed over the windows, making it pitch-black. In the morning light would filter through the cracks, and when the shutters were open a stunning view of the countryside would open up, with the ocean glistening beyond the rolling hills.

It didn't take him long to make the room ready, and then he went back to the car.

Emmeline was still asleep, and he knew the kindest thing to do would be to carry her inside and leave her to sleep.

But fire was raging through his body, tormenting him as much as it was her, and there was only one answer to that.

He opened her door and crouched down, hesitating for a second before pressing his lips to hers.

In her drowsy state, she opened her mouth to receive his and moaned, lifting her hands to curl them around his neck, her fingers twisting in the dark hair at his nape.

'Pietro…' she moaned, and he undid her seatbelt then lifted her out of the car in one easy movement. He cradled her against his chest, carrying her with grim determination into the house. He moved up the stairs at the front, through the corridor and then up the flight of internal stairs.

'Where are we?' she asked, looking around and then, as if remembering that she was annoyed with him, pushing at his chest. 'I can walk.'

'I'm aware of that.'

He shouldered the door of the bedroom open and Emmeline looked around, a soft gasp escaping her lips. Dozens of candles had been lit, casting a golden glow in the room.

The *bedroom*.

Music was coming from somewhere, a lilting song in his native language that did something strange to her heartbeat.

He placed her down on her feet with care and then straightened, catching her face between his hands. 'You have two choices, Emmeline.'

'And what are those?'

'You may use this room to sleep,' he said softly, stroking her cheek. 'Or we will be together here tonight. Your first time. *Our* first time.'

He dropped his lips to hers softly, studying her, waiting. He felt as if he'd been waiting an eternity already...

CHAPTER SEVEN

THE AIR STRETCHED between them, thin and tense. Emmeline's heart was rabbiting about in her chest. She'd wanted this for a *really* long time. Since their wedding? Or since her father had first suggested this harebrained idea?

The thought of marriage to the charismatic tycoon she'd adored from afar for as long as she could remember had scared the heck out of her—mainly because she'd known she'd find it impossible not to fall head over heels in lust with the confirmed bachelor.

And love? Would sleeping with him blur the lines of what they were, just as he'd said? And was she brave enough to reject him when he was offering something she wanted so badly?

She blinked up at him, doubt making her voice quiet. 'I'm not tired.'

He expelled a breath he hadn't realised he'd been holding.

'Thank God for that.'

And now his patience deserted him.

He balled a hand into her hair, tilting her head back to allow him access, and kissed her as she'd never been kissed before. His tongue duelled with hers, lashing her with his need, and his body was hard and erect as he pushed her backwards onto the bed. She fell and he went with her, lying on top of her as his kiss pressed her head into the mattress and her body writhed beneath him.

A fever of need was spinning from her womanhood through her whole body, making her pant with desperate hunger. And he understood it. It burned in him, too.

'This is so beautiful,' she gasped, watching the candlelight flickering against the wall, casting shadows that did something to her insides.

'*Si.*'

His hands pushed at the fabric of her dress, lifting it higher, moving it up her body, exposing her long legs to him so that he groaned into her mouth as he felt the expanse of her thigh.

'*You* are beautiful,' he added, dragging his mouth lower, teasing the flesh at the base of her neck.

After a lifetime of not wanting to be beautiful it was strange for her to find those words so seductive, so pleasing. She swallowed.

He flicked the pulse point in her neck that was pounding hard and fast, his tongue a call to arms she couldn't ignore. Her hands pushed at his jacket and he groaned low in his throat as she arched her back at the same time, needing more, so much more, wanting her to touch him, to feel him.

Despite her complete inexperience she was driven by an ancient feminine dance, the power of which had been implanted into her soul at birth.

She rolled her hips, cursing the fabric between them. But his length was hard and it pressed against the sensitive flesh of her need. He thrust it towards her as though they were naked. He ground it against her and heat rose inside her. Her eyes had stars dancing in front of them and her breasts were tight, her nipples straining against the fabric of her dress, desperate for attention.

He ran his palms over her flesh and she cried out at the unexpected touch. As he ground his arousal tighter, harder, faster, his hands moved over her breasts and an orgasm split through her, its intensity almost ripping her apart.

She arched her back, moaning, crying out, her hands pushing at his shirt as the strength of the feelings he'd stirred made breathing, speaking, *anything* almost impossible.

But Pietro wasn't close to finishing. He was going to make this a night Emmeline Morelli would never forget. A night worthy of her first time.

As her breath softened and her cheeks glowed pink he crawled down her body, his hands worshipping her through the dress, his mouth running over the soft folds of fabric until they connected with her underpants. They were simple white cotton, and that brought a smile to his face. He liked to imagine her in them. That alone would fuel his fantasies for years to come. But for now they served no purpose.

He slid them down her body, over the shoes she still wore, discarding them at the foot of the bed. She was writhing, her body still on fire. He traced circles along her legs with his fingers, moving towards her thighs.

She gasped, and the sound made him smile.

'You want me to touch you here?' he said softly, padding a thumb over the sensitive cluster of nerve-endings.

'I want everything,' she moaned.

His erection jerked hard in his pants. As hard as it

could, anyway, when it was already taking up more room than was left inside the fabric.

'You are going to get it,' he promised darkly.

His hands were gently insistent as they separated her legs, pushing them wide apart to reveal her whole self to him. Before she could guess what he intended to do he ran his tongue across her seam.

She cried out into the room as new pleasures began to swirl around her, but he held her legs still, keeping her open to him. Keeping her right where he wanted her.

It was both an invasion and a sensual adventure. The intimacy of the act should have embarrassed her, or shamed her, but it did neither. She tilted her head back and stared at the ceiling as his tongue lashed her sensitive nerve-endings and euphoric delight careened over her body. She was at the top of a rollercoaster and the ride was only just getting started.

Emmeline didn't try to control herself as cry after hoarse cry came from her mouth. She couldn't. She was completely subjected to the pleasure he was creating. He was her master.

'I want you to come,' he said against her body, and the words were a command that started a fever inside her.

She reached up and grabbed the duvet in her fingers, wrapping her hands around it and arching her back as his tongue moved faster, deeper, harder. Finally the muscles deep inside her squeezed hard, wet and desperate, and then, overjoyed, she felt pleasure fill her. It rioted through her, ricocheting off her body.

'God…' she whimpered at the candles in the room, shivering and yet covered in perspiration at the same time. 'I can't believe you just did that.'

His laugh was slightly unsteady as he dragged his mouth higher, over her flat stomach to her gently rounded breasts. He flicked one nipple with his tongue and then moved his mouth to the other, clamping his teeth over it just hard enough to make her cry out with renewed awareness.

'Why can you not believe it?' he prompted, his smile lazily indolent, his eyes hooded as his head came level with hers.

'I just… You kissed me…down there.'

'Down *here*, you mean?'

He curved a hand possessively over her womanhood and she sucked her lip between her teeth, nodding slowly.

'I want to do that again and again,' he promised, the heel of his hand pressing on her flesh just hard enough to keep the tremors of sensation going.

'Okay.' She smiled up at him, her body strangely lethargic in the midst of the passion he'd stirred up.

His laugh was a rumble…a coarse sound. He stood up, and for a moment she was assailed by loneliness and concern. *Was he stopping?*

But his fingers flicked at his buttons, loosening his shirt, pushing it off his body to reveal the full expanse of his tanned naked chest. She'd seen him like this before—in the pool—and the memory of that had burned itself into her fantasies.

But this was different.

He was undressing for *her* now. Undressing with his eyes hooked to her body, his fingers moving with determined speed as he slid the clothes from his body until he was in just a pair of black briefs. His arousal was evident through the fabric, straining against it, pushing outwards so her eyes couldn't help but be drawn to it.

'Am I right in thinking you have not *seen* a man before, Emmeline?'

The question was asked impassively, with no judgement, but Emmeline's face flushed with blood. Embarrassment made her look away and swallow.

'Of course I've seen a man,' she said quietly.

'Naked?' he prompted.

She shook her head, still unable to meet his eyes.

'Come here.'

Her heart thundered inside her body but she stood, closing the small distance between the bed and him. Even her own nakedness didn't shame her, though she'd never been this way before.

As if instinctively understanding her thoughts, he caught her around the waist. There was something in his expression—a confusion, a newness—that made her breath hitch in her throat. He drew her against the hard planes of his body and she made a soft sound of anticipation as his arousal pressed against her.

'I didn't want to marry you,' he said thickly. 'But now I can't think of anything I want more than what we are about to do. You are…uniquely beautiful.'

The words made her heart flutter; it felt weightless, without gravity, and she felt it might lift out of her body altogether.

'I'm not.' She shook her head.

'You try to disguise your beauty,' he corrected. 'And I cannot understand why, when most women do everything they can to enhance what they have.'

For a moment pain lanced her. A pain so deep, so embedded, that it had always been a part of her.

'It's who I am,' she said quietly.

'I want to get to know who you are,' he murmured. 'I didn't want to marry you, but you're my wife. And I'm glad.'

Her stomach churned and emotions ransacked her body, filling her heart with something new.

A sense of belonging.

He caught her hands and lifted them to his underpants. 'Undress me.'

Her eyes flew to his; doubt and uncertainty warring with temptation. 'I've never done this…' she babbled.

He laughed softly. 'I'm aware of that.'

She drew her brows together, her face a mask of doubt. 'I thought educating virgins wasn't your thing?'

'Not just any virgin,' he said in a gravelled tone. '*You*, Mrs Morelli.'

'What if I'm not…? What if this isn't…?' She closed her eyes, forcing herself to think clearly and speak what was on her mind. 'You told me you're used to experienced lovers. What if I'm terrible in bed?'

That unfamiliar stroke of guilt slashed through him anew. *He'd* said that. In fact he'd said words to that effect several times. Why had he been such a bastard to her?

'Tonight I want to show you what your body is capable of,' he said thickly, pulling her closer and making her gasp when his arousal throbbed hard against her body.

He felt her knees tremble. Her eyes were huge in her face, all honey and caramel, awash with far too many thoughts and doubts. Doubts *he'd* put there. Doubts he wanted to remove one by one, kiss by kiss.

'I'm scared,' she said, with such simple honesty it broke his heart.

'I know.' He kissed the tip of her nose.

His tenderness made her heart swell. Her fingers moved of their own accord, pushing at his underwear, lowering it over the hard line of his erection and then down, over his thighs. He stepped back, moving out of his underwear as he guided her to the bed.

She fell backwards, but he didn't immediately join her. Instead he reached into the drawer beside the bed and pulled out a foiled square.

'Protection,' he said with a half-smile.

'Ah. No grandkids.'

She nodded, her wink reminding him of the first day they'd discussed this marriage. When she'd been so sure of herself. Sure that she was getting a convenient husband, a ticket to her university studies and to…freedom. The word lodged in his mind as incongruous, as it had done back then.

'Not tonight.' He grinned.

Their eyes met and the air sparked with something neither had ever felt before. Though Pietro had slept with more women than he could easily remember, he'd never taken a woman's virginity. Even as a young man he had gravitated towards experienced lovers. This was new ground for them both.

How could he reassure her? Drive that doubt from her mind properly?

A strange sense of uncertainty ached in his gut. But she pushed up on her elbows and stared at him.

'I want this,' she said with soft confidence. 'I don't care what happens next. I want to *feel* this.'

He nodded and lowered himself onto the bed, kissing her slowly, sensually, marvelling at the feeling of flesh on flesh. Her naked breasts were flattened by his hair-roughened torso. His arousal was close to her—so close he could take her. The way she was trembling beneath him was a reaction to the newness of this, even as her eyes looked at him as though he was the air she needed to sustain life.

He dragged his mouth lower, rolling one of her nipples with his tongue while his hand slid down and splayed her legs wide, giving him more room, more access.

'You tell me if you need time,' he said thickly, not even sure the command made sense.

But she understood. She understood as though he'd spoken in a language made just for them.

She nodded and he lifted his head, one hand cupping her cheek as he kissed her hard. His tongue was passion and flame and she writhed beneath him, lifting her hips, searching for him, welcoming his invasion.

And God knew he wanted that too.

He pushed into her gently, gliding only his tip into her warm, tight core, giving her time to adjust to each incremental sensation as he filled her anew.

She moaned into his mouth as he moved, and all his control was required to stop himself taking her as he wanted to—hard and fast. He pulled out slowly, then pushed in deeper, before removing himself again. As he did so each time he took more and more of her and her muscles relaxed, welcoming him deeper, without restraint, without reserve, until he was pressing against the barrier of her innocence.

He kissed her, holding her tight as he thrust past it, removing it forever, imprinting himself on her as the first lover of her life. The first man who'd touched her like this.

Finally his whole length was sheathed by her, wrapped up in her, squeezed by her, and he paused, giving them both a moment to adjust to how it felt. He pushed his face higher so he could see her properly, could read her face. He saw wetness in her eyes and something turned in his gut.

'You're in pain.'

He moved to pull out of her but she shook her head and wrapped her legs around his waist.

'No, no, it's…' She shook her head and her smile was tight. Self-conscious. 'It's fine.'

Perfect, she amended inwardly. Everything about the moment was more perfect than she could ever have fantasised or hoped. It was sublime.

'"Fine" is a good starting point,' he said darkly. 'But it requires improvement.'

And then he moved quickly, his body thrusting into her and pulling out, each movement sparking an electrical current beneath her skin until she was almost out of breath. The assault on her senses was unlike anything she'd expected. Even when he'd touched her and brought her to orgasm it had been different from this. Now every nerve-ending in her body was twitching, as though he was stirring her from the inside out.

And he was, she realised, arching her back as the feelings began to overtake everything.

The galaxy was bright and hot and she was intimately aware of her part in it: like flotsam, bright and floating, powerless and yet powerful. A contradiction in her heart.

She dug her nails into his shoulders as wave after

wave of pleasure swallowed her, devoured her, making her eyes leak hot tears she didn't even feel. Only when he caught one with his tongue and traced it up her cheek did she realise she was crying—but she couldn't stop.

She was incandescent, the explosion of her pleasure like a fire in her blood. He held her as she came, held her tight, reassured her, whispered to her in Italian, his words stirring her up more, hotter, faster. She clung to him as the tornado swirled around her, held him as though he alone could save her, and then she cried out, sweat beading on her brow as the storm broke.

Pleasure saturated the room, thickened her breath. She clung to him until the craziness slowed and she was once more herself.

But she was not herself. She'd never be herself again. She had shaved off pieces of her being and handed them to him, bound them into his soul and his flesh, uniting herself with him even if he didn't want that.

She fell back onto the bed. The beauty of what they'd shared was incredible. Yet it was almost immediately eclipsed by a sense of guilt. Of self-doubt.

She'd just experienced the most unimaginable delight and he...he'd simply had a good workout.

'I'm sorry,' she muttered, turning her face away and staring at one of the flickering candles. 'I told you I wouldn't be any good at this.'

'Hey.'

He caught her face in his hand and turned her back to look at him, even though she couldn't bear to see the pity and disappointment in his eyes.

'What are you talking about?'

'Nothing,' she muttered.

It was impossible to give voice to the embarrassment that was quickly usurping her delight. Uncertainty and inexperience were horrible accomplices, and they dogged her every thought.

'Cara...' He spoke quietly, bringing his mouth to her earlobe and pulling it between his teeth, wobbling the flesh and breathing warm air over her delicate pulsepoints so that she shivered anew. 'Do you feel this?'

He thrust into her again, deeper, harder, his body like a rock.

'Yes, but you didn't—' She bit down on her lip.

His laugh was soft recrimination. 'I did not finish because I didn't want this to be over. Believe me, it is taking every ounce of my willpower not to.'

Her eyes clashed with his, trying to read truth in his statement.

'You answer my needs perfectly,' he promised.

She wasn't sure she believed him, but then he began to move once more and she was lost to thought. She arched her back, her body held by his, and this time as he rocked her to new heights of awareness and fulfilment his mouth tormented her breasts, so there were fires raging in every part of her body.

She ran her fingers over him, wanting to touch and feel every inch of him, to enjoy his body as he was hers. And as she began to fall apart at the seams, a tumbling mess of sensation and feeling, a tangle of emotions, he kissed her, his mouth holding hers as he made her world shift once more.

Only this time he came with her.

Feeling him throb inside her, feeling his body racked by a pleasure he couldn't control and knowing it was being with *her* that was doing that to him made an ancient feminine power rock her. She held him tight and kissed him back, her mouth moving over his as he lost control of himself, as though she felt he needed some kind of reassurance.

Later she would find that instinct absurd, but in that moment it filled her, made her desperate to comfort him somehow.

He swore in his own language, the harsh epithet filling her mouth and her soul.

'You were worried I wouldn't enjoy myself?'

He rolled away from her, pulling out of her and sitting up in one motion. His face was angled down towards her, his smile bemused.

'How do you feel?'

Emmeline blinked up at him and stretched her body. She was covered in a fine sheen of perspiration and her nipples were taut; there was a red rash on the parts of her body his stubble had grazed, including her thighs, and at the top of her legs. She arched her back, tossing her arms over her head and stretching like a cat in the sunshine.

'I feel…*whole*.' She smiled and closed her eyes, her breathing soon deep and soporific.

He studied her for a moment, hearing the reality of what they'd done banging on a door in his mind—one he was going to ignore for as long as possible.

'Tell me,' he said thickly, running a finger over her abdomen up to the swell of her breast.

'What?' She flicked her gaze to him.

'Explain to me why you haven't done that before.'

'Maybe I was waiting for you,' she murmured, the words incongruous in their sweetness. She broke the spell by smiling teasingly. 'Or maybe I just didn't meet anyone who tempted me.' She pushed up on one elbow, her eyes not shying away from his. 'Is that so strange?'

'Yes.' He shook his head. 'Yet it also makes sense.'

Her eyes dropped to the sheet between them. 'I'm glad you made an exception to your "no virgins" rule for me.'

His laugh was a soft caress. 'That was rude of me.'

'It was *honest* of you,' she corrected, stretching again, her body lean and long and begging for his touch.

He cupped her breast possessively, his eyes simmering with tension as they locked to hers. 'Do you need anything? Food? Water? Wine? Tea?'

She shook her head slowly. How could she need anything when he'd just made her feel like that?

She smothered a yawn with the back of her hand and he smiled.

'Sleep, then.'

'Mmm…but then I might think this was all a dream.'

He covered her with the duvet that was folded across the bottom of the bed. 'Which will give me the perfect opportunity to remind you otherwise,' he said, with a deep husk to his words.

Her eyes were closed, her breathing even, but she was still awake. He watched as she breathed in and out, her face calm, her cheeks still pink from the heat of their lovemaking. He watched as the smile dropped and her wakefulness gave way to slumber…as her breathing grew deeper and steadier and her eyes began to dance behind their lids. Her lashes were two sweeping fans across her cheeks.

And still he watched. Without realising it he was being pulled into a spell; it wrapped around him, holding him immobile.

There were mysteries surrounding his bride. Mysteries of her choice. Her being. The contradiction that lived deep inside her. She was stunningly beautiful and yet she did everything she could to hide that fact. She had lived like a prisoner for years—a prisoner of her father's love and concern, but a prisoner nonetheless—and yet she was brave and spirited, strong and independent. Why had she sacrificed her independence for so long?

She was sensual and desirable and yet she'd never even been kissed. How had she subjugated that side of her nature for so many years? She was twenty-two years old but she lived like a Victorian. Most women her age had their heads buried in their smartphones, sending glamorous selfies to their social media followers. She read books by the pool and covered herself from head to toe. *Why?*

These were questions to which he badly wanted answers, but there were other overriding questions that poisoned the perfection of the moment.

How would she react when she learned the truth about her father's health? Would she be able to forgive him for keeping it from her?

And, most importantly of all, why did the idea of lying to her, disappointing her, inadvertently hurting her with his dishonesty, make his skin crawl all over?

CHAPTER EIGHT

HER BODY THROBBED in an unusual new way. She stretched in bed, and wondered at the strangeness of everything. Not just her body, but the smells that enveloped her. Sort of citrus and lavender, clean and fresh. And the sounds—or lack of sounds. No busy motorways or bustle of a nearby city.

Her eyes blinked open, big pools of gold in the darkened room—dark save for the flickering of a couple of candles and the glow of a laptop screen beside her.

'Ciao.'

His voice was a warm breath across her body. She looked up at Pietro—her husband...her lover—and a lazy smile curved her lips.

'I had the strangest dream,' she murmured, pushing up onto one elbow so that the duvet fell from her body, uncovering her breasts for his proprietorial inspection.

He dropped his eyes to the display, unashamed of enjoying her nakedness. 'Are you sure it was a dream?' he prompted, folding his laptop closed and placing it carelessly on the bedside table nearest to him.

'It must have been,' she said softly. 'It was too perfect to be anything else.'

She was so beautifully unsophisticated. He couldn't

remember the last time he'd been with a woman who didn't dissemble in some way. Her honesty was as refreshing as her body was tempting.

He brought his frame over hers, so large against her slender fragility that Emmeline couldn't help but feel safe in his presence. As though nothing and no one could hurt her if he was by her side.

The thought evaporated when his lips touched hers, his kiss perfection in the midst of her body's awakening.

'I want you again,' he said.

Her smile was broad. 'Good.'

He dropped his eyes for a moment. Something was clearly bothering him.

'I want you too,' she reassured him.

His laugh was a kernel of sound—a husk in the night. 'I hated seeing you with those men.'

She blinked, having no idea at first who he was talking about. Then, 'I was just talking.'

'I know that.' His smile was self-deprecating. 'It is possible that I overreacted.'

She burst out laughing. 'Is that some kind of extremely hesitant apology?'

He ran a hand over her hair, stroking its dark glossy length thoughtfully. 'Yes.'

'Apology accepted. But, Pietro? You can't really expect me never to speak to another man...'

'*Lo so.* I know.'

'Good. Because I came to Rome to find my feet—to be myself. I can't do that with you getting all shouty every time I have an innocent conversation with someone...'

'I know.'

He lifted himself up and straddled her, the strength

of his want for her evidenced by the rock-hard arousal that was already pressed against her abdomen.

'But I will bring you to my bed each night and make it impossible for you to even *think* of another man.'

He dropped his head, placing a kiss on her temple.

'I will be all you think of and your body will crave mine.'

He thrust into her without warning and she cried out at the sweetness of his invasion, the possession that she was already hooked on.

'Starting now.'

'Starting a couple of hours ago,' she corrected breathily.

He grinned. 'Yes.'

He made love to her as though she was his only lover—as though he'd been dreaming of her for years. As though he needed her and only her. He made love to her with an intensity that blew her mind and filled her with the kind of sensual heat she hadn't believed could possibly exist.

She refused to acknowledge the truth: that she was one of many lovers for him and he was her only.

Afterwards, as she lay with her head resting on his chest, listening to the strong, fast beating of his heart and feeling the steady rise and fall of his chest, all was silent in the bedroom.

Except for the rather loud and insistent rumble of her stomach.

She burst out laughing, self-conscious but mostly amused. 'Apparently I'm starving.' She sat up straight, turning her face towards his. 'I hardly ate today,' she said after a moment, thinking back to her shopping trip and then the time she'd spent styling her hair and applying make-up.

'Why not?'

He stroked a hand over her back as though it was the most natural thing in the world, and his touch stirred a deep sense of rightness right down in the bottom of her soul.

She chewed on her lower lip. 'Just busy, I guess. I don't suppose there's anything here though…?'

'If so then someone's going to find themselves out of a job tomorrow.'

'Why?' she asked, looking around the darkened room. Only a few candles remained alight, flickering lazily against the white walls.

'Because I retain a full-time housekeeper to maintain this estate.'

'Estate? What *is* this place?'

His hand stilled on her back and then resumed its contact, as though he couldn't bear not to touch her. 'It is what you would call a bolthole,' he said after a small pause. 'My own little slice of the world.'

'Why would you need a bolthole, Mr Morelli? Is it for when your hordes of admirers and past lovers get too much?'

It was meant to tease him, but his face flashed with true annoyance. 'There is significant media intrusion in my life—something you might have noted if you'd been with me more.' He winced at the way that had sounded and shook his head. 'Sorry. I'm sure you're no stranger to that sort of invasion.'

'No,' she agreed, and she wasn't offended or upset— only interested. 'Though staying on the plantation as often as I did meant I wasn't really a figure of much interest,' she said quietly, conveniently glossing over the articles that had been so painful to her teenaged heart. The articles that had so callously compared her boring appearance to her mother's legendary beauty.

'You're lucky,' he said, taking her statement at face value. 'For years I was followed everywhere I went, with paparazzi eager to catch a photograph of the kind of mess I'd get into next.'

His wink hid genuine pain; she wasn't sure how she knew that, but she did.

'Including your escapade with that very much married Brazilian model?'

He grunted. 'Apparently.'

She expelled a soft breath—a sigh that meant nothing. It simply escaped her lips without her knowledge.

'I didn't know she was married,' he surprised her by saying gruffly. 'We didn't have that kind of relationship.'

She nodded thoughtfully. 'What kind of relationship *did* you have?'

He looked at her thoughtfully for a moment and then pushed out of the bed, striding across the room and grabbing a pair of shorts.

'You don't want to talk about it?' she asked as he pulled them up his body, leaving them low on his hips.

'I'm happy to talk about it if you would like. But let's get you something to eat as we speak, hmm? I don't want your energy fading.'

She hid her smile and stood, keeping a sheet wrapped around her as she moved.

His laugh was mocking. 'Why are you covering yourself?'

She sent him a droll look. 'Because I'm naked.'

'And you are worried I might see you?' He crossed the room, dislodging the sheet from beneath her arms, dropping his head to kiss her shoulder. 'Really? After what we've shared?'

Her cheeks flushed pink and something inside Pietro twisted painfully. So her innocence wasn't just a question of virginity. It was simply *her*. She had a sweetness, a naivety that was so unusual he doubted he'd ever seen anything like it.

'*You're* wearing something.'

'Yes, but I don't look like you.' He grinned, pulling her close. 'I want to *see* you.'

'Believe me, I feel the exact same way.'

His laugh was a little off-kilter, but he stepped backwards and slowly slid his briefs from his body so that he was completely naked.

'Better?'

Emmeline felt as though she'd eaten a cup of sawdust—her mouth was completely dry. 'Uh-huh.'

He laughed, kissing her cheek, and then reached for her hand. He laced his fingers through hers and she grinned.

'What?' he asked.

'First time I've held hands with a guy. Other than my father.'

He pulled a face that perfectly covered the way his heart was rabbiting about like a wild thing in his chest. 'I don't want to think of your father right now.'

Or the fact that he had cancer. Was dying and lying to his only daughter. Nor the fact that he was using Pietro to cover that lie.

Emmeline's laugh covered the unpleasantness of his thoughts. 'Sorry. It's just this is all so strange.'

'*Si. Quest'e verita.*'

He pulled her after him, out through the door and down the stairs, and for the first time Emmeline spared a thought for the dwelling they were in. It was a very unassuming rustic farmhouse. Large terracotta tiles lined the hallway and the walls were cream. The furniture was nice, but certainly not designer.

'It came like this.' He answered her unspoken question.

'When did you buy it?'

He squeezed her hand. 'Here.'

He guided her into a kitchen and lifted her hand to his lips, kissing it before releasing her fingers from his grip. He opened the fridge and she watched, waiting.

'Five years ago.'

'Why?'

He thought about not answering, but what was the point in that?

'I'd broken up with a girlfriend. The press thought we would get married. So did she, I suppose. It was a messy split. Acrimonious. Bitter. Public.' He grimaced. 'I learned a lot from that experience. Most of all the importance of having somewhere to go when things get heated. I should have taken the time to calm down.'

'You didn't?'

He shook his head, pulling a box out of the fridge and opening it. 'I stayed in Rome.'

'That was bad?'

He laughed. 'I did a lot of drinking to forget her. A *lot*. It was not a good phase of my life.'

'I'm sorry,' she murmured, hating the lash of jealousy that whipped her spine.

'Don't be. We are still friends, and I realised that I

needed somewhere all to myself. No one knows about this farmhouse. It's owned by my corporation, but I never bring anyone here.'

Pleasure soared at the fact that she'd made the cut, but there was envy too. 'How...*admirable* that you're still friends.'

His eyes met hers, his smile making her feel as though she'd been sledged in the gut. 'Jealous?'

'Not at all.' She looked away, hating how transparent she must be to him. Unfortunately she had no experience in pretending not to give a crap about her husband's past. Especially when his past must so radically outstrip her own experience.

'Why does that annoy me?' he mused, lifting a piece of meat out of the container and placing it on a dark timber chopping board. He reached for a knife; it glinted in the light.

'I don't know,' she said softly, distracted by the motion of the knife as it cut easily through the meat. 'Even with this place you're still in the press more than I can ever imagine.'

'And you are *never* in it,' he said thoughtfully, placing the pieces of sliced beef onto a plate and then turning back to the fridge.

'Well, there's nothing interesting about me,' she said softly.

'That isn't true.' A frown tugged at his lips. 'You are an anachronism.'

'I know.'

She couldn't help it. She reached over and lifted a piece of meat, placing it into her mouth just as he turned around.

Her eyes met his and she shrugged. 'I'm starving,' she said through a full mouth.

He grinned. 'I'm glad to see you eating. You need energy.'

Her pulse raced. 'Do I?'

'Oh, yes, *cara*.'

He paused, his eyes scanning her face so intently that she froze.

'What is it?'

'When you smile like that you look so much like your mother.'

Something flashed in her expression. Something that was definitely not pride or pleasure. It was doubt. Guilt. Pain.

Curiosity flared in his gut. 'That annoys you?'

'Of course not,' she said stiffly. 'My mother was very beautiful. I'm flattered.'

'No, you're not.'

'Why do you say that?'

'Because I know you,' he said simply.

And her stomach flopped because she didn't doubt he was being honest.

'So why do you not want to look like Patrice?'

'You'll never be like me! Take this off! Wipe it all off! It's too much rouge, too much mascara. You look like a porn star gone wrong.'

Emmeline shuddered, her smile as fake as the night was dark. 'You're wrong,' she insisted, even as the memory scratched its fingers over her spine.

'I'm never wrong.' His eyes sparked with hers. 'But I can be patient.'

He placed a handful of strawberries on the plate, then a wedge of cheese and some bread.

But I can be patient.

Did he have some mysterious super-ability to know just what she needed to hear?

'It's complicated,' she said, after a moment of silence had passed.

'Family stuff often is.'

His smile showed a depth of experience that she understood.

'Are your parents pleased you've "settled down"?' She made inverted commas with her fingers and he lifted his broad shoulders.

'I suppose so. Rafe thinks you're quite irresistible,' he added as an afterthought. 'I think he's more than a little jealous that your father chose *me* as your groom *du jour.*'

Emmeline made a sound of amusement and lifted a strawberry to her lips. Strangely, she was not remotely self-conscious in her nudity. Everything about that moment felt right.

'Have you ever been in love?'

Except that.

The question came from her lips completely unexpectedly, uninvited and unwanted. He stared at her for a moment, his expression unreadable.

'No.'

'Seriously?'

She reached for the plate but his hand caught hers, lifting it to his lips. He pressed a kiss against her palm and then took her finger into his mouth, sucking on it for a moment. Her stomach rolled.

'Seriously,' he murmured, coming around the kitchen bench to stand opposite her.

'But you've been with so many women.'

'Sex isn't love, *cara*.'

Just like that the floor between them seemed to open up; a huge hole formed and it was dark and wide...an expanse of confusion and heartache that she couldn't traverse.

Sex isn't love.

And it wasn't.

Sex was just a physical act. A biological function. A hormonal need.

Nothing more. Why had she asked that stupid question?

'What about that woman you broke up with? The one the press went into a frenzy over?'

'Which one?' he muttered, arching his dark brows.

'Five years ago—before you bought this place.'

'Bianca,' he said quietly. 'I cared for her. I still do.'

Jealousy was no longer just a flame in her blood; it was a torrent of lava bubbling through her, burning her whole.

'Bianca as in that beautiful redhead you were all over at our wedding?'

Contrition sparked inside him—and regret too. He'd forgotten that Emmeline knew her name. It was a stupid, foolish oversight that Pietro would never ordinarily have made.

'That was wrong of me.'

'You can say that again,' she snapped, reaching for a pistachio nut as a distraction. 'You're still seeing her?'

Her insides ached. Her body still throbbed with his possession, her nerve-endings were vibrating with the awakening he'd inspired, and she was jealous. So, *so* jealous.

'No.'

Emmeline stood up. She felt strange. Strange and achy.

'It's none of my business,' she said quietly, moving around to the other side of the kitchen bench—ostensibly to grab some more food, but in reality because she needed space.

'Of course it is. You're my wife.'

'But this isn't a *real* marriage, remember? We have a deal. You're free to…to do what you want.'

He stared at her long and hard. 'You don't think that's changed now, Emmeline?'

Doubts flickered inside her. 'What are you saying?'

'I don't want to see anyone else.'

He hadn't even realised that himself, but as he stared at his beautiful bride he knew it was the truth. And he knew she deserved to know it.

'I want to sleep with *you*. A lot. I want to be married to you. And I know we are doing this all the wrong way around, but I want to get to know you. There is so much of you that is a mystery to me, and for some reason I have become obsessed with uncovering all your secrets.'

He came around to her side of the bench and dug his hands into her hips.

'Every. Single. One.'

'This place is so beautiful.' She stared out at the rolling hills of the countryside, her eyes clinging to the fruit orchard in the foreground before moving on and landing on the glistening ocean. 'I don't know how you can ever leave.'

'Business,' he said simply. 'My office can't actually function for that long without me.' He thought of the emails his assistants had been forwarding and grimaced. 'I have to get back.'

Emmeline sighed. 'Today?'

'Now,' he agreed.

Or soon, he amended, sitting on the spot of grass beside her. After three days in the countryside he wasn't sure he could put off the reality of life for a moment longer. He wanted to, though.

'But it's so nice,' she said again, tilting her head to look at him.

She rested her cheek on her knees, which were bent against her chest, and he had to fight against reaching out and touching her. It was his 'go to' impulse now, and he suspected he might need some kind of 'Emmeline patch' to get through a day in the office without her.

How had he ever thought her ordinary and dull to look at? She was so breathtakingly beautiful that he derided himself for not having noticed. It didn't matter what she wore—these past three days she'd gone around in old shirts of his and she'd looked sexier than any woman he'd ever known.

No, she was simply Emmeline.

He saw every expression that crossed her face—including the slight flicker of regret that shifted her lips downwards now.

'You can stay here,' he said quietly. 'I can come back on the weekend. If you'd prefer it…'

'No.'

The response was instantaneous. How could she stay away from him? Her addiction was firmly entrenched. She couldn't remember a time when his body hadn't taken over hers.

'We'll come back some other time.'

She stood a little jerkily, wiping her hands across her knees.

He followed her and got to his feet, then caught her around her waist. 'I'm glad we came here.'

'Me too.'

Her smile was bright, but there was something in her expression that he didn't like. An uncertainty he wanted to erase.

Only he had no idea how.

He'd spent three days with her but he hadn't uncovered a single secret. Instead, he'd got to know her body intimately. He'd become acquainted with every single one of her noises, every single movement her body made that signalled pleasure, need, desire, an ache. He'd learned to read her body like a book, and yet her mind was still an enigmatic tangle of uncertainty...

'You seem nervous.'

She flicked her gaze to him, wondering at his perceptive abilities. 'I guess I am.'

Her smile was tight. Forced. Anxious.

Pietro slowed the car down, then pulled off to the side of the road. Emmeline's gaze followed a young child skipping down the street, his mother walking behind, her arms crossed, her eyes amused.

'What is it?'

Emmeline shifted her gaze from the child—his mother was next to him now, her smile contagious.

'Honestly?'

'Si, certamente.'

'It's stupid.'

'I doubt it,' he said reassuringly, his voice low and husky.

The statement was a balm to her doubts. Still, she hesitated before she spoke.

'What happened back there...' She bit down on her lip and cast a glance over her shoulder, towards the road they'd just travelled at speed. 'The closer we get to Rome, the more it feels like a fantasy. Like it never really happened. Like it won't happen again.'

'How can you say that?' he asked, a genuine smile of bemusement on his face. 'I was there. It happened. It happened a *lot*.'

Pink spread through her cheeks and she looked away, uncomfortable and disconcerted. 'But it doesn't feel real, somehow.'

He expelled a soft sigh. 'It *was* real.'

She nodded, but her uncertainty was palpable. 'I guess it's just...the last time we were in Rome everything was still so weird between us.'

His laugh caressed her skin.

He pulled back into the traffic, his attention focussed ahead. 'A lot's happened since then.'

And it had—but the fundamental truth hadn't changed, except in one crucial way. It was weighing on him more and more, heavy around his neck. Knowing that her father was dying and that she had no idea was an enormous deceit now. They'd crossed a line; they were lovers.

But Pietro wasn't overly concerned. Of the many things he excelled at, one of his strengths was managing people and situations. He just had to manage this situation tightly. Starting with his father-in-law.

CHAPTER NINE

'YOU DO NOT sound well,' he drawled down the phone, wondering at the sense of anger he felt towards this man he'd always admired and respected. A man he loved. A man who had helped him remember himself after the despair of losing his own father.

Col's cough was a loud crackle. 'I'm fine. The goddamned nurse is here, taking my temperature.'

'Rectally?' Pietro's response was filled with impatience. He softened it with a small laugh. 'Because you sound cranky as all hell.'

'I am. I'm a damned prisoner in this room.' Another cough. 'How's my girl, Pietro? Are you looking after her?'

Again, a surge of annoyance raged through Pietro's chest. 'She doesn't appear to need much looking after. Emmeline is stronger than I'd appreciated.'

Col's laugh was broken by a wheeze. 'Ah. I see you've come up against her stubborn side. Try not to judge her too harshly for it. She inherited that from me.'

'Mmm…' Pietro nodded, rubbing his palm over his stubble. He should have shaved. The pink marks of his possession had become regular fixtures on Emmeline's skin.

'Is there a problem?' Col's question was imbued with the strength that was part and parcel of the man.

'*Si.*'

'What is it? She's happy, isn't she? You told me you'd look after her…'

'She's happy,' Pietro agreed, thinking of her flushed face lying beneath him, her eyes fevered, her brow covered in perspiration. Then he thought of her uncertainty as they'd driven back to Rome the day before. The way she'd seemed pursued by ghosts unseen.

'So? What is it?'

'She deserves to know the truth about your health,' Pietro said heavily. 'She isn't going to understand why you haven't told her. You must give her a chance to see you. To say goodbye.'

A wheeze. Then another. Pietro waited, but his loyalty was shifting from the dying man to his daughter—the woman who loved her father and had no idea his life was ending.

'You can't tell her.'

It wasn't the response Pietro had expected. He shifted his weight to the other foot and braced an arm against the glass window that overlooked the city. In the distance he could make out the hill that screened his villa from sight. Was she there, looking out on the same blanket of stars he was? Was she staring up at the sky, wondering about him, missing him, wanting him?

His body throbbed with a need he fully intended to indulge. *Soon.*

'Someone has to,' he said, with a soft insistence that was no less firm for being quietly spoken. 'She deserves to know.'

'You aren't to say anything.'

Col's voice was raised, and in the background Pietro heard someone—a woman—telling him to calm down.

But Col was working himself up, his tone harsh. 'If I'd wanted her to know I'd have damned well told her. She's my daughter, Pietro. You've known her for a month—I've known her all her life. I know what she needs, damn it. You can't ruin this.'

'She deserves a chance to say goodbye.'

'No.' It was emphatic. 'I'm already gone. The man she thought I was…the man I used to be…that's not me now.'

There was a thick, throaty cough, then the scuffling sound of the phone dropping to the floor.

Pietro spoke quickly. 'Col? *Col?*'

A woman's voice came more clearly into the earpiece as the phone was lifted. 'Hello?'

Pietro expelled an angry breath. 'Yes?'

'I'm sorry, Senator Bovington needs to rest now. This conversation will have to wait.' The nurse lowered her voice. 'And next time please take more care not to upset the Senator.'

The call was disconnected before Pietro could ask to speak to Col for a moment longer. He shoved his cell phone back into his pocket and paced to the other side of his room.

And he swore, loudly, into the empty office, his temper ignited more than ever before.

The confidence he'd worn into the office earlier was morphing into doubt. Emmeline deserved to know the truth, but it wasn't Pietro's confidence to break. Perhaps with anyone else, he would, but Col was like a second father to him. He wouldn't share this secret until he had Col's permission. He couldn't.

But the knowledge that he was lying to Emmeline was a weight on his chest, and he found himself hesitant to go home to her that evening. The idea of looking at her, kissing her, making love to her, knowing that he was sitting on such a fundamental secret, made his situation unpalatable, to say the least.

He dialled Rafe's number on autopilot.

'Ciao?' Rafe answered, the single word slightly rushed and breathless.

'Are you free for dinner?'

'What time is it?'

Pietro gazed down at his gold wristwatch. 'After seven.'

'Dio. Already?'

'Si.'

'Okay. Dinner in an hour?' He named a restaurant near his own apartment. 'Is Emmeline joining us?'

Pietro's spine ached with rejection but he shook his head. 'Not tonight. She has…something on.'

Rafe was silent for a moment. 'You've always been a bad liar. I'll meet you soon.'

He disconnected the call before Pietro could refute the claim. Then he flicked his cell phone from one hand to the other and finally loaded up a blank message.

I have a meeting to attend. I'll be late. I'm sorry.

He grimaced as he sent it. Rafe was right; Pietro was a God-awful liar.

He saw the little dots appear that showed she was typing a message, but they went away again almost instantly, without any message appearing. He frowned, waited a few more moments and then put his phone back into his pocket.

Rafe was waiting at the restaurant when Pietro appeared.

'So?'he asked, nodding towards the martini that was sitting at the empty place on the table. 'What's going on?'

Pietro took the seat and threw back half the drink in one go. 'I need your complete discretion,' he said quietly, his tone showing the seriousness of his mood. 'This is a…a *private* matter.'

'Of course.' Rafe was clearly resisting the urge to joke about feeling like an extra from a bad World War Two resistance movie. He must sense it was not the time.

'Col's sick.'

'Col? Col Bovington?'

'Yes. Who else?' Pietro hissed.

'What do you mean, sick?'

'He has cancer; it's terminal.' He paused, in deference to the memories he knew would be besieging Rafe of the cancer that had taken their own father. 'He has months to live. Perhaps only weeks.'

'Poor Emmeline. She must be beside herself. I know how close they are.'

'Yes.' Pietro nodded angrily, his jaw clenched as he reached for his drink and twisted it in his hand. 'The thing is, she doesn't know.'

'She doesn't *know*?' Rafe repeated with disbelief, his dark eyes latching on to his brother's. 'What the hell do you mean?'

'Col wanted it that way,' Pietro responded with a defensive lift of his shoulders. 'And when I agreed to keep it from her I didn't… I hardly knew her,' he finished lamely. 'I didn't think it would be any hardship not to tell her the truth. I didn't care about her at all.'

'And now?' Rafe pushed.

The newness of what he was feeling was something Pietro wasn't willing to ruin by discussing it, though. He kept his answer vague.

'I know her well enough to know that she'd want the truth. She wouldn't want Col going through this alone. She'd want to be with him at the end.'

'Perhaps.' Rafe nodded. 'But Col is obviously seeking to protect her from the grief of watching a much-loved parent die...'

'We've been through that. But aren't you glad we got a chance to say goodbye to our father? To honour him? To ease his suffering?'

'We aren't Emmeline. If Col is right—and you must assume he knows his own daughter—then you'd be hurting her for no reason. And Col would never forgive you.'

'No. I gave him my word.' Pietro's response was stony. Cold. His heart was iced over by the thought of how that promise was betraying Emmeline. 'Until he frees me from that obligation I must keep it.'

'It sounds to me as though you've made your decision,' Rafe murmured gently. 'So what do we need to discuss?'

Pietro glowered. What he needed was for someone to absolve him of guilt, to tell him he was making the right decision. But no one could do that—and very possibly he wasn't.

'*Niente.*'

Emmeline turned the page of her book, having no idea what she'd just read. In truth, she'd covered several chapters, but she couldn't have recounted a single incident that had taken place.

Where was he?

And who was he with?

Her heart twisted in her chest as she thought of her husband with someone else. What assurance did she have that he wasn't still seeing Bianca, or any number of his past lovers?

Doubts filled her, making her feel nauseous and exhausted.

She should have gone to bed; it was late. But waiting for him to come home had become an obsession. She didn't want to fall asleep—to have him return at some point in the middle of the night and for her body to respond to his when he might well have been...

God. Was he sleeping with someone else?

A car's engine throbbed outside the door, low and rumbling, and her tummy flopped as her eyes looked to the clock. It was just after midnight.

Butterflies danced inside her, beating their wings against the walls of her chest, and her fingers were shaking as she flipped another page.

The door was pushed inwards and she waited, her eyes trained on the corridor beyond. Waiting, watching. He didn't see her at first. His head was bent, his manner weary. He stood dragging a hand through his hair, staring into space.

'Oh. You're home!' she said, in an admirable imitation of surprise.

He started. His eyes flew to Emmeline's and she knew she wasn't imagining the darkening of his expression. The look of something in his face that might well be guilt.

'I didn't expect you to be awake, *cara*.'

'I've been reading. I guess the book engrossed me,' she lied. *What was it even called?* She folded it closed carefully, without attempting to stand. 'Did you have a good night?'

There it was again! That expression of uncertainty. Of wrongdoing. Her stomach churned and she looked away, unable to meet his eyes but knowing she had to speak honestly about how she felt. She needed to know where she stood.

'Have you been with another woman?' The question was a whisper. A soft, tremulous slice of doubt in the beautiful lounge of his villa.

'Oh, Emmeline...' He moved quickly to her and crouched down at her feet. 'No. Of course I haven't.' He put a hand on her knee, drawing her attention to his face. 'I had dinner with Rafe.'

'Yes.' She nodded jerkily. 'I know. He called hours ago, to say you'd left your jacket at the restaurant. He said he'd drop it by later in the week.'

Hours ago. Pietro understood then why his wife was so uncertain.

'I had to go back to the office to finish something,' he lied.

He'd needed to think. And he hadn't been sure he could face his wife with the knowledge he held—the lie he was keeping from her. What had seemed so simple was now burning through his body, making each breath painful.

'You can't seriously think I would be seeing anyone else?'

'I don't know,' she said softly, her eyes not able to

meet his. 'I mean, I knew what I was getting when I married you…'

'No, you didn't. Neither of us did,' he said simply. 'I thought I was marrying the boring, spoiled daughter of a dear friend. I didn't expect my wife to be *you*. I thought I'd want to carry on with my life as before…'

'But you don't?' she pushed, her eyes huge as finally they met his.

'Not even a little bit,' he promised. He stood, holding a hand to her. 'You have to trust me, Emmeline.'

Guilt coursed through him. How could he ask that of her?

Emmeline bit down on her lip. She trusted Pietro with her life, sure, but her heart…? And it was her heart that was involved now. Her whole heart. It had tripped into a state of love without her knowledge, and definitely without her permission, and she couldn't say with any certainty that he wouldn't break it.

Not intentionally, but just by virtue of the man he was.

'Trust me,' he said again, cupping her face. 'I don't want anyone else.'

'It's crazy,' she said softly, doubt in her features. 'We only just met…'

He dropped his mouth to hers, kissing her with all the passion in his soul. She moaned into his mouth, wrapping her arms around his neck. So much for not responding, she thought with an inward snort of derision. She couldn't be in the same room as her husband and not feel as though a match had been struck.

'We've known each other for years.'

He kissed the words into her mouth and they filled up her soul.

'But not really.' She pulled away, resting her head on his chest, listening to his heart.

'I remember the first time I saw you,' he said quietly. 'I'd come for your mother's funeral. You were a teenager, and I think even then I knew that I was looking at you in all the wrong ways.' His smile was apologetic. 'You had just come home from school, do you remember?'

Remember? Of course she remembered. Her father's handsome young friend had looked at her and a fire had lit in her blood.

'Yep.' She cleared her throat. 'You were the most gorgeous person I'd ever seen,' she said with mock seriousness. 'You fuelled *all* my teenage fantasies.'

His laugh was a soft rumble. 'No wonder you never met a boy you liked,' he teased. 'Who could live up to *me*?'

It was a joke, but Emmeline was falling back in time, her mind tripping over those painful years in her life.

She covered the direction of her thoughts with a flippant response. 'Who indeed?'

'I thought at the time that it was strange you were still at school. Your mother had just passed away, and yet you were carrying on with your life…'

'People handle grief in different ways,' she said softly. 'I needed to be around friends. The familiar. Sophie was a godsend.'

'How come you've never told your father what you know about Patrice's death?'

She looked up at him, her eyes awash with emotions. A part of him—the part of him that wanted his wife to be happy and at ease—felt he should back off. But the rest of him—the part that so desperately needed answers—pushed on with his line of enquiry.

'He thinks you believe she simply crashed.'

'She did crash.' Emmeline's smile was tight, her tone dismissive.

'But she drove into that tree on purpose.'

'Probably drunk,' Emmeline said, with the anger she tried so hard to keep a tight rein on taking over for a moment.

She stepped away from Pietro, pacing towards the window that overlooked the city. Her eyes studied its beautiful glow but she hardly saw it.

'Why do you say that?'

'Because she was always drunk at the end.' Emmeline bit down on her lip but the words were bubbling out of her almost against her will.

Pietro frowned. 'Your father has never mentioned that. There was no hint of it in the media.'

'Of course there wasn't,' Emmeline said wearily. 'Daddy controls the local press, for the most part. *And* the coroner's office.'

Emmeline spun around to face Pietro, bracing her back against the glass window behind her.

'If she'd hit another car, hurt someone, then I don't think even Daddy would have been able to keep it hushed up. But as it was only Mom died, and no one could have gained anything from seeing our family name disgraced.' She swallowed, her throat a slender pale column that was somehow so vulnerable Pietro ached.

'How do you know about her drinking?' Pietro murmured.

Emmeline swallowed, looking away. Years of silence kept her lips glued shut even now.

'How do you *know*?' he insisted, staring at her lowered face, waiting for her to speak.

'Because she couldn't hide it towards the end. She was a drunk. A *mean* drunk,' she added quietly.

Pietro's eyes narrowed. 'Mean, how?'

Emmeline expelled a shaking sigh. 'Just mean.'

'To you?' he prompted.

'Of course. With Daddy away at the Capitol for much of the time, I was the only one around to *be* mean to. Well, other than the servants—but they were paid well and put up with it.' Emmeline swallowed back the sting of tears and pressed her palms to her eyes. 'I could never do anything right by her.'

She shook her head angrily.

'Everything about me offended her. Especially as I got older. I remember there was one dinner and Congressman Nantuckan made some throwaway comment about how beautiful I was, that I was going to be every bit as pretty as my mom when I grew up. I must have been all of twelve. He was probably just being kind,' she said, shaking her head. 'But Mom was furious. *Furious*. As though I'd planned some elaborate betrayal and laced her dinner with cyanide.'

A dark and displeasing image was forming for Pietro, but he took care not to react visibly. 'What did she do?'

'Nothing. Not straight away, anyhow. Mom would never show her hand publicly. But once everyone left she pulled all the clothes out of my wardrobe. She told me I was on the right track to becoming an A-grade whore if I didn't watch out. She—'

Emmeline gasped as a sob escaped her, and lifted a hand to her mouth to block it.

'I'm so sorry,' she said, shaking her head desperately.

'I never talk about this! But I've ripped off the Band-Aid and I don't seem able to stop…'

'I don't want you to stop,' he assured her, fighting the urge to close the distance between them. He wanted to comfort her, but he suspected that it would cause her to stop sharing, and he desperately wanted to understand more about her life.

She nodded, but her hands were shaking, and finally Pietro gave up on maintaining his distance. He walked to the bar and poured a stiff measure of Scotch, then carried it to his wife. She curled her fingers around it, sniffed it before taking a tiny sip. Her face contorted with disgust and she passed the glass straight back.

'Yuck.'

His smile was indulgent, but impatience burned inside him. 'You were twelve, and on the cusp of changing from a girl into a young woman…?' he prompted.

She nodded, pulling at the necklace she always wore.

'She couldn't stand that. When I was young she was such an attentive, affectionate mother. We were very close. But from around ten or eleven, as I shot up and started to develop a more mature body… Mom saw it as some kind of act of defiance. She started to see me as competition, hated the time I spent with Daddy. When people came to the house she'd send me to my room. I wasn't allowed to wear anything that drew attention to myself. Cosmetics were forbidden. So was dying my hair or having it cut into a style.'

'Yet you were still beautiful,' he said softly. 'And anyone would have been able to see that.'

Emmeline's eyes met his with mockery. *'You* didn't. You specifically told me that I didn't look good enough to be your wife.'

He groaned—a sound of deep regret. He *had* said that. 'Emmeline, I saw you as a teenager. I wasn't thinking straight the night you came to my office. And, if anything, I suppose I was…annoyed.'

'Annoyed?' she prompted.

'*Si.* Annoyed that you went to such effort to cover up your natural beauty.'

'Even after she died it was a habit. I don't know… I guess I got very mixed up. Any time I would even *think* about wearing something other than what she'd chosen for me I'd hear her voice, hear the things she'd called me, and I'd know I could never do it.' Emmeline blinked, her enormous eyes round and golden in her face. 'When you told me I needed to change how I looked…'

'I was a bastard to say that to you,' he said gruffly.

'Yes. An *arrogant* bastard,' she agreed, although the words were softened by her smile. 'But you freed me, in a weird way. It was almost as if I'd been waiting for someone to shake me out of that mind-set. To remind me that she was gone and the power she'd exerted over me had gone with her. There was an article in the papers not long after she died. It compared me to her and the headline was *Dull Heiress Can't Hold a Candle to Dead Mother*. Can you believe that?'

His snort was derisive. 'Ridiculous journalists.'

'Yes, and a ridiculous story. They'd taken a heap of long-lens shots of me leaving school, playing baseball— you know, generally the worst, most unflattering pictures. A normal girl would have been devastated by that.'

'You weren't?'

'No. I saw it as a tick of approval. I was doing just what I was supposed to. Mom would have been proud of me.' She shook her head again. 'It took me a long time to unwrap those thoughts and see them for the idiocy they were. For many years I couldn't gain that perspective…'

His eyes swept closed and he processed what she was telling him. He thought of the way he'd criticised her appearance—first telling her she was too conservative and then accusing her of looking too 'available' when she'd dressed as he'd suggested.

'You are beautiful to me no matter what you wear—and to any man. Your mother was playing a foolish and futile game, trying to hide you like that.'

'She wasn't exactly firing on all cylinders,' Emmeline pointed out with a grimace.

'I cannot believe your father wasn't aware…'

'He doted on her,' Emmeline said wistfully. 'There was a significant age gap between them, as you know. She was his precious, darling wife.' She shook her head bitterly from side to side. 'He had no idea.'

'I can't understand that.'

Emmeline shrugged. 'I think it's quite common. A lot of people who love someone with a dependency issue fool themselves into thinking nothing's wrong. They don't want to admit the truth, so they don't.'

'But—'

'I know.' She lifted a finger to his lips, her smile distracting. 'It doesn't make sense.' She dropped her finger lower, digging the tip into the cleft of his chin. 'The first thing that's gone right for me is actually…um…'

'Yes?' he prompted, the word a gravelled husk.

'This. Marrying you. It must seem crazy to an outsider but here…with you… I feel so alive. For the first time in a long time I'm myself again. Thank you.'

Guilt was heavy in his chest.

Tell her. Tell her now.

He wanted to so badly, and there was only one way to stop the words galloping from his mouth. He crushed his lips to hers, taking possession of her mouth with his, pressing her against the window, making her his once more. Here, like this, everything made sense.

Nothing and no one—no truth kept or lie uncovered—could hurt what they were.

CHAPTER TEN

THE NIGHTCLUB WAS full to overflowing and the music was low-key, electronic. It thumped around the walls. The lighting was dim. Even dancing with her husband, his arms wrapped around her waist, she couldn't make out his face properly.

'So this is where our wedding guests came?'

He nodded. 'I believe so.'

His hands dipped lower, curving over her rear, holding her against the hint of his arousal. Her eyes flared with temptation and desire.

'It's nice…' She wrinkled her nose as she looked around, studying the walls that were painted a dark charcoal and featured beautiful black and white prints of Italian scenes.

'I am going to take a stab in the dark and say it's not your usual scene,' he teased, kissing the top of her head.

'Not exactly!' She laughed. 'But that doesn't mean I can't learn to like it.'

'There is no need. I don't come here often.'

'But you have something to do with it?'

'I financed it,' he agreed.

'Uh-huh. That would be why they treated you like some kind of god when you walked in here.'

'Or it could have been because of the incredibly beautiful woman on my arm.'

She shook her head, her smile dismissive. 'I'm sure I'm not the first woman in a nice dress you've brought through those doors.'

He slowed for a moment, hating it that she was right—hating it that his past was as colourful as it was. Not once had he questioned the wisdom of the way he lived, but now, married to Emmeline, he wished more than anything that he *hadn't* slept with any pretty woman who'd caught his eye. He wanted to give her more than that, but he couldn't exactly wind back time.

'Have you spoken to your father lately?'

'Ah...' She expelled a soft sigh. 'A change of subject, I see. I take it that means I'm the hundredth woman you've come here with, or something?'

He compressed his lips, angry with himself and, perversely, with Emmeline for pushing this line of enquiry. 'Does it matter?'

She blinked up at him and shook her head. 'I guess not.'

She looked away, but the pleasant fog of sweet desire that had wrapped around them dissipated. A line had been drawn and she'd stepped back over it, warily.

'I was just thinking,' he said gently, 'that I wish I had come into this relationship with less baggage.'

'Fewer ex-lovers, you mean?' she murmured, moving in time to the music even as most of her mind was distracted by the idea of Pietro *ever* making love to someone else.

'Si, certo.'

'But why?' she asked softly, and stopped moving, staring up at him.

'You deserve better than someone like me.'

He was surprised to hear himself admit that. Until that moment Pietro would have classified himself as supremely confident and self-assured.

'But perhaps you wouldn't be such a sensational lover without all those women you've been with before,' she quipped, winking up at him.

His laugh was gruff. 'So practice makes perfect?'

'Yes. But now you get to practice with just me.'

'And you are perfect,' he said quietly.

He kissed her gently then, and the world stopped spinning, the music stopped playing. Everything was quiet and still—a moment out of time. A moment that resonated with all the love in Emmeline's heart.

And in his too?

She didn't dare hope that he loved her. She knew that what they were was changing, morphing, shifting every day. That he looked at her as though he'd never seen a woman before. That he held her after they'd made love until she fell asleep. That he was always holding her, still, in the soft light of morning.

She knew that he was choosing to work fewer hours in his office and instead spending time in the villa. Oftentimes he was propping up a laptop, but generally near her. By the pool, in the lounge, in their bedroom.

And that was the other thing. Since they'd come back from the farmhouse she hadn't slept in her own room once. His room was becoming 'their' room.

Still… Getting close to one another was one thing. Falling in love was quite another. Emmeline wasn't going to get her hopes up. Life had taught her that there was safety in low expectations and it was a hard lesson to shake.

The song came to an end, fading seamlessly into another.

'Are you hungry?' he murmured into her ear.

She looked up at him, her eyes meeting his with sensual heat. 'Not for food,' she said quietly.

His laugh set her pulse firing. 'Then let's get out of here.' He squeezed her hand. 'I just have to see Leon—the owner. Want to come?'

'Not particularly.' She smiled at him and he smiled back, and the world was quiet again, spinning softly around them as if Emmeline and Pietro existed in their own little space. 'I'll wait in the car.'

'Five minutes,' he promised, holding up his hand and flexing his fingers.

She nodded, watching as he cut through the crowd effortlessly. Or did it part for him? Either way, he moved unencumbered through the hundreds of dancing guests. Once he was out of sight she turned and made her way in the opposite direction, towards the doors of the night-club.

'Emmeline.'

The sound of her name had her pausing, turning, a blank smile on her face as her eyes scanned the crowd. She didn't see anyone she knew at first, and was about to resume her progress towards the door when a beautiful redhead came into view.

And then she knew instantly who was looking back at her.

'Bianca.'

The woman's smile was bone-chilling. 'You know who I am? Good. That saves me the trouble of introductions.'

'I saw you pawing my husband at our wedding,' Emmeline heard herself say, and instantly wished she could pull the words back. They were rude and unnecessary, and the last thing she wanted was to make a scene.

'Being pawed *by* your husband is a more accurate description,' Bianca commented, with a purr in the words.

'Yes, well… That's ancient history,' Emmeline said, lifting her slender shoulders in what she hoped looked like an unaffected shrug.

'If that's what you want to believe,' Bianca said, her smile tight, her lips bright red. 'You know, I could *never* put up with a husband who was so easily tempted away. But then, yours is hardly a *conventional* marriage, is it?'

Emmeline's doubts, already so close to the surface, began to wrap around her anew. Her brain—logical, calm, cool—knew that Bianca had every reason to be unkind. That her gloating attitude was probably just a cruel manipulation aimed at hurting Emmeline. But the muddiness of what she actually was to Pietro, and the truth of what she *wanted* to be, made her heart ache.

'I almost wish *I* had married him,' Bianca said, tapping a fingertip along the side of her lips. 'But this way I get to have my cake and eat it too.' Her laugh was a soft cackle.

'I don't understand…'

'I get the best parts of Pietro—without the press intrusion and the expectations of being Mrs Pietro Morelli… You're good cover for him and me.'

Emmeline felt as if she was drowning.

She stared at Bianca and shook her head. 'I don't know if you're telling me the truth, or just trying to upset me, but either way it's time for me to go.' She blinked her enormous eyes, the hurt in them impossible to conceal. 'Please don't come near me again.'

'It's not *you* I want to be near,' Bianca purred as a parting shot.

Emmeline spun and made a beeline for the door, bursting through it and into the night air with an overwhelming sense of relief.

Pietro was only seconds behind her, his breath loud, as though he'd just run a marathon. 'Was that Bianca I saw talking to you?'

Emmeline didn't have time to hide the hurt in her eyes. She nodded bleakly, then looked around for their car.

A muscle jerked in Pietro's cheek just as a camera flash went off. He swore angrily and put a hand in the small of Emmeline's back, guiding her away from the nightclub towards his car. He opened her door without saying a word, then moved to the driver's side.

He revved the engine as soon as she was buckled in, and pulled out into the empty street. The silence prickled between them, angry and accusatory.

'What did she say to you?' he asked finally, as they cleared the more built-up streets of the city and went on their way to his villa.

'Nothing.' She frowned, then closed her eyes. 'I don't know if it matters.'

Pietro gripped the steering wheel until his knuckles glowed white. 'Tell me what she said.'

Emmeline swallowed, her mind reeling. She had gone from the euphoria of being with Pietro to feeling as if everything was a sinister ruse.

'She told me our marriage was a convenient cover for your relationship with her. She implied that you and she are still very much a thing.' Emmeline shook her head. 'She knows that our marriage isn't conventional.'

The words were a sharp accusation and Pietro swore.

'That last part is true,' he said thickly. 'I shouldn't have said anything to her but I was…angry. I was wrong to expose you to that kind of gossip.'

'Yes, you were,' Emmeline muttered, her heart plummeting. 'I'm sure she's told anyone who cares to listen,' she added, mortified.

'I don't care. It's not true any more. You *know* how much everything has changed between us.'

He reached down and put a hand on her knee but she jerked away. Her eyes lifted to his and the pain and uncertainty in them had him swearing and veering the car off the road, pulling to a rapid halt in a space marked for buses.

'Please listen, *cara*. You know the truth about Bianca and me because I have told you. She has always wanted more from me than I have to give. She is very jealous of you.'

'I know that,' Emmeline said quietly. 'And I know she wanted to hurt me tonight and obviously cares very much for you. But it makes me wonder… What do I know about *you*?'

'You know *everything* about me.' He groaned. 'Please believe me, Emmeline. I have never had with any woman what I have with you. This is special, and different, and you and I are both finding our way with it. Don't let outsiders—someone like Bianca—cause problems for us.' He pressed a finger beneath her chin, lifting her face to his. 'I won't let you. I won't let *her*.'

'I wish you didn't have such a long list of ex-lovers,' she muttered.

'None of them matters to me. Not a bit.'

Her eyes clashed with his; she wanted to believe him so badly. 'Have you been with her since we married?'

He shook his head.

'In that first month?' she persisted, holding his gaze. 'When we weren't sleeping together? I hardly saw you, and you were home late almost every night.'

He shook his head. 'I had dinner with her once. But that's all. I think I *wanted* to sleep with her. To prove to myself that our wedding hadn't changed anything. But the truth is I'd kissed you by then and I no longer wanted any other woman.'

Her heart turned over in her chest. Was it true? Did she believe him? It took such a leap of faith for her to trust anyone—especially given the strange circumstances. But gradually she found herself relenting.

'Why were you always so late?'

'You need to ask?'

His smile was like sunshine on a rainy afternoon. She felt its warmth penetrating the storm and could have wept with relief.

'I didn't trust myself not to touch you,' he said thickly. 'It was bad enough on our wedding night, when I kissed you and touched you and tasted your sweetness for myself. But after the night you wore that dress...' He groaned. 'I knew I was in serious trouble.'

The truth in his words filled her. 'Why couldn't you touch me?'

His smile was lopsided. And sexy as hell.

'Because you were meant to be a bride of convenience. Ours was an arranged marriage. I wasn't supposed to be craving you. To be dreaming about you... obsessing over you.' His sigh was exaggerated. 'And yet I was. I *am*. I suppose initially I resented that. I wanted to prove to myself that I could resist you. Spoiler alert: I couldn't.'

She expelled a soft sigh, but the memory of Bianca was still too fresh for her to relax completely.

'I don't want to see her again,' Emmeline muttered.

His eyes glinted with a heated emotion she couldn't interpret.

'Believe me, you will *never* see that woman again.'

'Can we go home now?'

He nodded, and inside he felt as though he'd been spared from Death Row with a minute left on the clock.

He dropped his head and kissed her slowly, gently. 'Don't let anyone come between us, *cara*. I cannot change the man I was, but you are changing everything about the man I *am*. The man I want to be.'

Her stomach squeezed with happiness. Because she knew he was telling the truth.

She trusted him implicitly.

It wasn't long before they found their way back to each other's bodies, exploring every inch available and sating their appetites.

'You are crying,' he whispered, chasing a tear up her cheek, depositing it back in the corner of her eye.

She laughed through a sob, shaking her head, wrapping her hands around his waist. 'I'm sorry. It's just so perfect. I don't know what happened—what I did to deserve this—but it's just...'

He smiled—a smile that tipped her world off its axis—and then he thrust deeper, and she moaned into the cool night air, her body moving with his. They were completely in sync, completely together.

He kissed her as he ground into her and she wrapped

her legs around his back, holding him close, needing him in her core. His tongue lashed hers and together they spiralled off the edge of the earth in a tangle of limbs, sheets, sweat and cries.

Afterwards he stroked her hair, his eyes smiling down into hers. He rolled onto his back, pulling her with him, holding her tight, and she listened to the beating of his heart for a long time. She thought for a moment that he'd fallen asleep, but after a long time he spoke.

His voice was a gravelled husk in the night. 'Have you spoken to your father lately?'

'No.'

She shook her head and her hair tickled his nose. He patted it down flat and then stroked her naked back, feeling every bone of her spine, knotting down to the curve of her rear.

Tell her. Tell her.

But the moment was so perfect. Some time he might find a way to be honest with his wife. But on this night, with the sound of their lovemaking still heavy in the air, he couldn't bring himself to do it. To ruin what they'd just shared.

'You don't speak often? That's interesting. I would have thought you'd find being apart from him more of an adjustment.'

Emmeline shrugged. 'I lived on the plantation but my father was often away. I did try to call him a few days ago and he emailed back. Something about house guests.' She shrugged. 'That will mean he's out showing off the horses, the cattle, his shooting prowess.' She wiggled her brows—he felt the movement against his chest. 'Knowing Daddy, he's never been happier.'

Pietro groaned inwardly. The lie was tightening around his chest.

'My father speaks of you often, you know,' she murmured, apparently having no clue that her husband was in a self-induced hell of sorts. 'He adores you.'

Pietro's smile was tight. 'It's mutual.'

'Why?' She pushed up on her elbows to study him. 'Why are you so close?'

That bleak time from his past sat like a weight on his chest. 'I've always admired him.'

'That's not the same thing.'

'No,' he agreed. 'Years ago, I was in negotiations with your father. I was buying some commercial real estate of his—just off the Champs Elysées. I was devastated by my father's death—I got the call about it while we were in a meeting—and your father... Col... supported me. Not just that day, but afterwards too. I'd always admired him as a businessman, a politician, but as a friend he was irreplaceable.' He shrugged. 'He was a rock when I badly needed one.'

As Pietro spoke the words they reverberated around his soul. Col had been his rock when there'd been no imperative on him to be any such thing. He had been strength and resilience, and he had imparted those qualities to Pietro.

How could he be anything but loyal to the statesman now, in his own time of need? Pietro owed Col his allegiance, even though lying to Emmeline was beginning to poison him.

'That's just like him.' Emmeline smiled. 'He's so selfless...'

CHAPTER ELEVEN

'GOOD MORNING, MRS MORELLI.'

He dragged a finger down her body, finding her womanhood and brushing against it possessively. She writhed beneath him, remembering the way they'd made love the night before. Her body still throbbed from the strength of that pleasure.

'*Buongiorno.*' She blinked up at him.

'Do you know what today is?'

Her smile was irrepressible. 'My first day at university.' She grinned. '*Yay!*'

He laughed. '"Yay"?'

'Uh-huh. Yay. Just…*yay.*'

He dropped his head and kissed her gently. 'Which means we have been married two months.'

'And it feels like two weeks.' She stretched her arms over her head. 'Time really does fly when you're having fun.'

His wife—his beautiful wife—stared up at him with all the goodness in her soul and he felt as though the sun was beaming right through his chest.

'Are you nervous?'

'Nervous? God, no. I'm excited. I have been wanting to study for so long, Pietro. I can't believe I've put this off. I feel like there's a whole world out there—a world of learning and knowing—and finally it's going to be mine.'

She sat up excitedly, pushing the covers off her naked body and stepping out of the bed. He watched as she strolled across the room, uncaring of her nakedness. She pulled a pair of jeans off a hanger, and then a cream blouse, and took his favourite pair of briefs from her underwear drawer.

He groaned across the room. 'Not those.'

The smile she threw over her shoulder was pure impish cheek. 'Oh, yes. You can imagine me in them all day.'

'I'll imagine stripping them *off* you all day,' he corrected.

'That too.' She winked, sashaying into the adjoining bathroom and switching the fan on with the light.

The noise droned in the background and Pietro fell back against the mattress, staring up at the ceiling fan that was spinning lazily overhead.

The sense that he was betraying her had lessened. So, too, the feeling that he was living on borrowed time. After several more attempts at getting Col to tell the truth to his daughter Pietro had been forced to accept that the secret was there and that it existed beyond Pietro's control. They would deal with the fallout when it happened.

It never once occurred to him that there might be a fallout bigger than they could handle, because he and Emmeline had become a single, unified force. The idea of anything happening to them that they couldn't handle was impossible to contemplate.

He listened to the running of the shower and the

soft singing that she did without even realising. Smiled wider when he caught the tone-deaf notes she seemed always to miss.

He stepped out of bed, strode across the room and pushed the door inwards. Steam swirled around him. She had her eyes closed, her face lifted towards the showerhead, and water was raining over her face and down her back. She hummed now, quietly, and he grinned as he pulled the shower door open and brought his mouth down on hers without warning.

Her eyes flew open and then she surrendered to the kiss, moaning as he pushed her back against the cold tiles, groaning as his body pinned hers and water ran over them both, down their faces and into their mouths.

'Remember what I said the night you were talking to those two professors?'

He asked the question as he brought his mouth down to take a nipple between his teeth and roll it gently, as he moved his hand lower, brushing over her feminine core, before he transferred his mouth to her other breast.

'No...' she moaned, rolling her hips, inviting him in. Needing him again.

How was it always like this for them? Would it ever not be? She felt as if an explosion had caught her in its midst, powerful and fierce.

'I will bring you to my bed every night, so that no other man ever, *ever* interests you.'

The passion in his words was wrapping around her, squeezing her, filling her with all the love in the world. 'You already do that,' she said huskily.

'It never hurts to take precautions, though, does it?'

She laughed, but any hint of amusement died inside her as he dragged his lips lower, falling to his knees so that he could kiss her in her most sensitive, private place. His tongue ran along her seam and her knees quivered as sensations began to drown her, to make thought impossible.

'I can't believe there was a time when you were not mine,' he said against her flesh, and she moaned, running her fingers through his hair as pleasure spiralled in her belly, driving through her, making her blood heat and her heart pound.

'I need you!' she cried out as an orgasm began to unfurl, spreading through her limbs, making them weak and aching.

'I'm glad.'

He didn't stop, though. His fingers dug into her hips and he held her where he needed her, his tongue dictating the speed of her release, and the intensity too. She cried out into the shower as the orgasm unfolded, her mind exploding, every conscious thought obliterated by the havoc he wreaked on her body.

He kissed her quivering flesh as he stood, but didn't give her even a moment to recover. His hands spun her easily—she was weakened by the total meltdown of her bodily awareness—and he bent her at the hips. Holding her steady, he drove into her from behind and felt her tremble as his possession was complete—the ultimate coming together.

He throbbed inside her, his fingers massaging her wet, soapy breasts, his arousal rubbing against her sensitive nerve-endings, squeezed by her tight, wet muscles. He spoke in Italian—words that meant nothing and everything. He bent forward, kissing her back as he moved, stroking her, touching her, and finally, when her muscles squeezed him with all their need, he emptied himself into her, the feeling of ownership more complete than ever before. She owned him, and she was his.

Emmeline pressed her flushed face against the shower tiles, her mind reeling.

'I am going to find it very hard to concentrate today,' she said thickly, rolling her hips as he continued to pulse inside her, his length experiencing the aftershocks of the earthquake of their coming together.

'That makes two of us.'

He ran a finger down her back before easing himself out of her, away from her, releasing them from the agony and ecstasy of what they had been. She stood and turned to face him, and her eyes were so vibrant and her smile so broad that a dull ache spread through his chest.

He'd been fooling himself in pretending the lie didn't matter.

It did. Of course it did.

He ran a hand over her hair, wet and dark. 'Emmeline...?' he said softly, studying her cautiously.

'Mmm?' She wrapped her hands around his waist, holding him close to her body.

How could he tell her now? On her first day at university? It would derail her completely, and he'd already done his best to do that. No, he couldn't do it today.

But Col Bovington was going downhill, and enough was enough.

Pietro had an obligation to his wife. Soon, when the time was right, he would tell her.

Having made the resolution, he felt a thousand times better. As if simply by deciding to do something he had in some way enacted a small step of the deed.

Absolution was close at hand.

* * *

Emmeline hummed as she moved about the kitchen. There was a pile of textbooks in the corner, opened to the page she had most recently been reading. She cast a gaze over the *papas di pomodoro,* smelling the piquant sweetness of the tomatoes and the undertones of basil and garlic, then shifted her focus to the quails that were roasting in the oven.

It was the first time she'd cooked dinner for Pietro's family and she wanted everything to be perfect.

He'd laughed when she'd said as much. 'I have a housekeeper, a chef and a valet. Why do you not leave the food to them? You have too much on your mind already,' he had said, nodding towards the books that were littered around the house.

'I've only been at uni a week; it's still early days.' She'd smiled back. 'Besides, I want to. I like to cook and I think... I don't know... It just feels like something nice to do.'

Of course now she was regretting that impulse, as time marched on and food simmered and she worried that she would have nothing ready by the time they arrived.

There was nothing she could do but wait. The quail in *confit* needed an extra hour before they would be ready to remove. The soup was the entrée. There were olives, breads and cheeses ready to serve as antipasti.

She rubbed her hands together, checking the table for the tenth time. She'd set it with a simple white cloth and put several vases of old-fashioned roses in the centre. Sprigs of orange blossom lent them a beautiful fragrance. Plus, they reminded Emmeline of his farmhouse—the place where their relationship had come alive.

She smiled as she leaned down and breathed in deeply—then her back pocket vibrated. She reached down and fished her cell phone out, relieved and surprised in equal measure to see a text from her dad. She'd left several messages for him in the last week, and apart from a brief email she'd heard nothing.

Hi, Pumpkin. Sorry I've been hard to catch lately. I've got the flu and it's kept me in bed all week. Are you doing good? Love, Daddy.

A smile tickled her lips. It was something he had often asked her when she was younger.

I'm doing real good, Daddy. Uni is amazing.

She ran her finger over the phone, wondering what she should say about her husband and settling for, Married life suits me. Come over and visit soon?

She thrust her phone into her pocket and continued with her preparations. But as she showered and changed she couldn't help but let a kernel of worry infiltrate her happiness.

Her dad wasn't a young man. For the flu to have kept him in bed all week sounded serious. That and the fact that she hadn't spoken to him in rather a long time had her mind unpleasantly distracted.

She chose a black silk slip dress, teamed it with a long string of pearls and a pair of black ballet flats, then quickly applied basic make-up.

Pietro appeared just as she was bent forward, slashing mascara over her brows, and his eyes locked to her rear before she straightened and spun around.

'If it isn't my favourite husband,' she murmured, her eyes clashing with his in the mirror.

'Your *only* husband?' he prompted.

'For now.'

She winked and turned her attention back to the mirror, ignoring the serious tremble that assaulted her heart. Initially she'd felt their marriage would be of short duration. That she'd wean herself off life at Annersty, let her father adjust to her departure and then move on. For good. But now…?

'I have something for you,' he said softly.

Curious, she spun around, scanning his outfit, his hands, and seeing nothing.

'It's downstairs.'

'What is it?'

'Come and see,' he murmured, holding a hand out to her.

Emmeline walked to him, wanting to peel her dress off as she went, to expose her nakedness to him. She followed behind him, her curiosity increasing with each step, until they reached the front door.

He lifted his hand to cover her eyes. 'Wait a moment.'

She bit down on her lip, held her breath and listened as the heavy timber door was pulled inwards. Then his hand dropped from her eyes and she blinked, focussing beyond him.

A sleek black car sat before her. A Bentley with a soft roof that looked as if it would turn the car into a convertible.

'It's…it's beautiful,' she murmured. 'I don't understand…'

'Well, *cara*, you are a Roman now. You go to university here. You live here.'

He moved to the car and opened the driver's door; she followed, a frown etched in her face.

'Do you know what I have been thinking about lately?'

'What?'

'When we first discussed marrying, I remember you saying something about wanting only the freedom it offered.' He cleared his throat. 'I didn't understand it at the time. I still don't. But I know I want to give you everything in this world, and a car seems like an important step to true freedom.'

Unexpected tears sparkled on Emmeline's lashes. 'Stop doing this to me!' She groaned, a laugh breaking the seriousness of her mood. 'You're *too* perfect.'

'*Cara*, I'm not...'

Something flickered in his face—something that briefly made her heart skid to a stop before she pushed the doubts away.

He *was* perfect. She had no reason to worry that he'd ever disappoint her or let her down. He was her match in all ways.

'Thank you,' she said softly.

'Hop in,' he replied, and grinned.

She smiled brightly as she slid behind the wheel. 'You know, I'm not actually a great driver...'

His laugh was husky. 'Then I shall have to teach you.'

As he'd already taught her so much. 'The thing is, I get bored,' she said honestly. 'I find it all a bit dreary.'

'Not here, you won't. Roman roads are fun. They are designed to test you.'

'I love my car. Even if I just sit in it to study.' She grinned at him.

A plume of dust from further down the driveway heralded the arrival of another car, and Emmeline stepped out with true regret. As she did so she saw a university parking permit on the dashboard, and that single gesture of thoughtfulness meant more to her than the extravagant gift of such an expensive car.

'I love it,' she said again, walking around the bonnet and pressing a kiss to his cheek.

His eyes latched to hers and she had the strangest feeling that he wanted to say something else. That something was bothering him.

'Is everything okay?' she asked searchingly, her eyes scanning his face.

'Ciao, ragazzi!'

Pietro's mother stepped from the car, a vision in green, her hair styled in a topknot, a large gold necklace at her throat and a pair of gold espadrilles snaking up her legs. She sashayed towards them as though the driveway were actually a chic fashion show catwalk.

'Mother,' Pietro drawled, kissing Ria on both cheeks before she transferred her attention to Emmeline.

'Ah! My lovely daughter-in-law,' she said in her heavily accented English. 'Still too skinny, I see,' she said, with a disapproval that Emmeline guessed was only half joking.

'Mother,' Pietro scolded warningly. 'That is enough.'

'What? I want grandchildren. Can you blame me?'

Emmeline's heart squeezed painfully. The truth was, the image of a baby had begun to fill her dreams. How sweet it would be to grow their own little person in her body—to hold it and feed it and cuddle it and love it.

Maybe one day that would happen. But for now Emmeline was having her first taste of life as a normal adult woman and she wasn't ready to sacrifice her independence yet. Her life with Pietro was perfect and new, and she didn't want to add a baby into the mix.

Yet.

Her eyes met Pietro's over Ria's head and she smiled; she knew he understood. He wanted her to be happy. To be free.

Her eyes drifted to the car, and as they walked into his home, she saw the number plate: *Mrs M.*

Her smile stretched broader, making her cheeks hurt.

Rafe arrived only a few minutes after his mother. They were sitting at the table sipping rosé wine, when he strode in, relaxed in pale trousers and a T-shirt.

'Ah, Rafe. Off the yacht, I see,' Ria said critically, but her smile showed nothing but maternal pride.

'*Ciao*, Mamma.' He grinned, doing the rounds and saying hello to his family. 'This smells wonderful. So you cook, too?' he demanded of Emmeline.

'A few dishes,' she said with false modesty.

Emmeline had always loved cooking. She'd spent as much time in the kitchen as possible—especially when Patrice had been on the war path. It had been the perfect bolthole. A spot where she could make dishes and enjoy the therapy that cooking and baking offered. She'd mastered croissants from scratch at the age of fifteen—just before her mother had died.

'Tell me again why *I* did not get to marry you,' Rafe grumbled good-naturedly, taking the empty seat beside Emmeline.

'Hush,' Ria said, reaching across and batting at Rafe's hand. 'She is your brother's wife.'

'Still… A man can dream.' Rafe winked at Emmeline, then reached for a handful of *grissini*.

'Leave some for the rest of us,' Pietro drawled, taking the seat on the other side of Emmeline and passing a glass of wine to his brother.

Beneath the table, Pietro's hand found Emmeline's knee and he squeezed it. She turned to face him. Their eyes met and sparks flew that Emmeline was sure everyone must surely see.

She smiled softly and then focussed on the story Ria was telling. Or tried to. But beneath the table Pietro's fingers moved steadily higher, until they were brushing her thigh, teasing her, comforting her, simply *being* with her.

'I'll get the soup,' she said after a moment, scraping her chair back and moving towards the kitchen.

'Would you like a hand, darling?' Ria called after her.

Emmeline shook her head. 'I'm in control.'

In truth, a moment to herself was essential. A single touch from her husband was enough to set her pulse skittering and stay that way. Was it possible that if she stayed married to him she was going to end up having a stroke?

The thought made her smile, but it also made something strange shift inside her.

If she stayed married to him?

Where had that come from?

She lifted four bowls out of the cupboard and ladled delicious soup into them, thinking about the arrangement they'd come to. Discomfort was like ice inside her. They'd never really talked about how long they'd stay married for. But everything had changed. The deal they'd made was surely redundant now. She was in love, and she was pretty damned sure he was too.

Which meant *what*, exactly? That they'd live happily ever after? Was that even what he wanted?

Uncertainty brought her happiness down a notch. Perhaps they needed to have a talk about that? A *Where are we going?* conversation...

She grated some fresh parmesan over the top of the soup, adding a glug of oil and few leaves of basil.

The thing was, they'd done everything in reverse. From her extensive experience with books and movies Emmeline had gathered that generally two people met, discovered they were attracted to one another, dated, fell in love and slept together, then moved in together or got married. But at some point before that crucial last step they discussed what they wanted. Where their future was going.

Could they discuss that now? Or would it be weird? Everything was so good she didn't want to ruin it.

With a small noise of frustration she lifted two bowls and moved through the kitchen and back into the dining room.

'Let me give you a hand,' Pietro said, as though he'd only just realised his wife would be ferrying four bowls on her own.

'Thanks,' she murmured, depositing the first in front of Ria before following her husband back to the kitchen. As she walked through the door he caught her around the waist and pulled her to him.

'I want to take you upstairs *now*...' He groaned. 'Why is my family here?'

She laughed, but her heart was thundering, her pulse racing. 'I don't know. It was a terrible idea. Let's send them away.'

'Definitely.' He kissed her hard and fast. 'A down payment,' he said with a wink.

'Good. I'll expect payment in full later.'

'How much later?' He groaned again, his expression impatient.

She kissed his cheek. 'Not long, I hope.'

The soup was a hit. She had been anxious about cooking such a quintessentially Italian dish for her husband's family, but they seemed genuinely to love it, and Emmeline had to admit it was one of her best. The quail was perfect, too. Served with some crispy potatoes and garlic-roasted green beans, it was an excellent mix of flavours and textures.

Pietro took over hosting after dinner, making espresso martinis in the lounge area that they progressed to.

Pietro had given her a car. That *meant* something. Not to mention his sweet sentiments about her wanting freedom. This marriage was so much more than either of them had anticipated. It was real.

'You're quiet,' Rafe remarked, taking the seat beside hers.

Whoops.

'And you look concerned. Is everything okay?'

Emmeline hardly wanted to have a deep and meaningful conversation about her marriage with her brother-in-law, so she scrambled for the easiest explanation she could offer.

'Oh, you know...' She smiled at him, her mind turning over quickly. 'It's my dad. He's not well, and it's hard to be over here and so worried about him,' she said with a shake of her head.

Rafe's surprise was obvious, but Emmeline didn't understand it, of course. 'He *told* you?'

'Of course he told me,' Emmeline said with a small frown of her own. 'It's hardly a secret.'

'Oh, thank God. I know Pietro's been tearing himself up about all this. It must be a weight off his mind that you know.'

Emmeline's look was quizzical. It was just the flu, and she'd only recently found out about it herself. 'How does Pietro know?' she asked quietly.

Rafe froze, apparently sensing that they were speaking at cross purposes. He sipped his martini, his eyes scanning the room. 'Um…'

'How does Pietro know what?'

Pietro appeared at that moment, devastatingly handsome in the suit that she loved so much. But Emmeline hardly noticed.

'How do you know my father is sick?'

CHAPTER TWELVE

SILENCE STRETCHED LIKE a piece of elastic. Then it stretched some more.

Emmeline tried to make two and two add up to four but it wasn't possible.

'Rafe just said you've known for a while. That it's been tearing you up,' she murmured. None of this was making sense.

Rafe swore, standing up and setting his martini glass down in one movement. He tossed Pietro a look of deep apology. 'I thought she knew.'

Emmeline stood up too, the movement unknowingly fluid. 'Knew *what*?' Her voice was louder. More demanding. The fear in it was obvious.

'Emmeline?'

Ria appeared at her side, and only with every single ounce of self-control in her body did Emmeline manage to calm herself. To offer her a tight, terse smile. But her eyes were haunted, her skin pale.

'Thank you for a lovely dinner. I think I should leave you to it now,' Ria said.

'Me too,' Rafe added quickly. 'Don't see us out.'

Pietro glared at his brother before dragging his attention back to his wife. It was quite possibly the worst manner in which this news could have been dropped.

'What the *hell* is going on?'

Pietro expelled a long, slow sigh. 'Sit down, *cara*.'

'I don't want a damned seat,' she responded caustically, her eyes flying around the room as if answers might suddenly appear. 'Well?' She tapped her foot, her arms folded across her slender chest.

'Rafe seemed to think you knew—'

'Daddy has the flu,' she answered sharply. 'But that's not what you're talking about, is it? Pietro? What's wrong with him?'

Fear was written across her beautiful face; her eyes were haunted by it.

'Your father *is* sick,' he confirmed.

Emmeline made a grunting noise of impatient displeasure. 'I've gathered that. What's wrong with him?'

A muscle jerked in Pietro's cheek.

'Is it serious?'

'*Si, cara*.'

'Oh, God.' She reached behind her for the sofa, collapsing into it wearily. 'What is it?'

Pietro crouched before her, his hands taking hers. 'He has cancer. Advanced and incurable.' He rubbed a thumb over her hand, across the soft flesh of her palm. His heart hurt with the pain in hers. 'I'm sorry.'

Tears fell down her cheeks, but shock was numbing her to their balm. 'I don't understand. When…? How…? Why didn't he tell me?'

'He wanted you to be happy. He wanted to *know* you were happy, to die knowing that you weren't going to be left stranded by the loss of your father. He wanted to know that you have other things in your life. Other people.'

'You,' she said quietly, pulling her hands free and rubbing them along her thighs. 'When did you find out?'

Pietro reached up and touched her cheek but she jerked away from him.

'When?'

It was a primal grunt. She was skinning the situation alive, trying to boil it down to just bones and fact.

'The day he came to see me.'

Surprise resonated through the room as though an atom bomb had been dropped. 'Before we were married?' she responded angrily, her voice high pitched and stringy. '*Before* we were married? You've known this whole time. Oh, my God.'

She stood up jerkily, looking around the room as though she didn't recognise it. As though it were simply a set and she an actress—a character in a play with no real meaning, no real plot. Nothing was real.

She blinked, clearing the confusion from her mind and trying her hardest to hone in on what mattered. There would be time to come to terms with Pietro's betrayal. But in that moment more was at stake.

'How bad is it?'

'He's dying,' Pietro said, the words thick and guttural. He stood slowly, but didn't attempt to move towards her. 'He told me it was a matter of months. If that.'

'No. I don't believe you.'

She stared at him, all her grief and confusion and the bereft state of her soul silently communicating themselves to Pietro.

'My father is… He's never sick.'

Pietro's expression was bleak. 'The cancer is through-out his body.'

The words were like strange sharp objects. She could barely comprehend them. Her daddy was ill? Why had he sent her away? Was he in pain? Was he lonely? The thought of him going through something like cancer without anyone to hold his hand brought a lump to her throat.

'And you let me stay here with you, knowing I had no idea? Knowing that my whole world—' She stabbed her hand into her chest, her eyes wild in her face. '—my father, my only family, was dying on the other side of the world? How *dare* you make that decision for me? How *dare* you lie to me like that?'

'He wanted it this way.'

'It doesn't matter! You should have *told* me!' she roared, turning her back and stalking out of the lounge.

She took the stairs two at a time, pacing down the corridor and into his room, which they'd been sharing for weeks. She pulled clothes out of the closet at ran-dom. Jeans, a few skirts, shirts… She had more clothes at home—she didn't need to pack much.

Home. Annersty. The words whispered through her with sombre realism.

'I couldn't tell you,' he said with muted anger in his words. 'What are you doing?'

'*Why* couldn't you?' She spun around to face him, her eyes accusing.

'He made me promise and I owed it to him to keep that promise.'

'Even knowing how it would hurt me?'

'I didn't want to do that,' he said thickly. 'You must believe this is true. I was in an impossible situation…'

'Damn it, Pietro.' The words reverberated around their room. 'Don't you *dare* talk to me about impossible situations! This wasn't impossible. It should have been easy.'

'Your father—'

'Yes, yes…' She waved a hand in the air, cutting him off. 'You've told me. He didn't want me to know. But what did *you* think?'

He froze, the question so direct that he hadn't expected it.

'You must have thought about it. Did you think I wouldn't care? Did you think I'd be able to forgive you this?' She zipped her suitcase with such ferocity that her nail snagged in its closure and she swore under her breath. 'You've been sitting on a time bomb.' She dashed a hand over her eyes, wiping away her tears.

He made a visible effort to pull himself together, straightening his shoulders and wiping his expression clean. 'You want to go to him?'

Her eyes bore into his. 'Of *course* I do. I would have gone to him weeks ago if anyone had told me what the hell was going on.'

'Good…fine,' he murmured. 'I'll organise my plane…'

'No.' She reached for her phone with fingers that shook. 'I'll book myself on the next available flight.'

Her meaning was clear. She didn't want his help.

'I have a jet at the airport. It will take hardly any time to fuel…'

'I don't want your stupid jet,' she snapped. 'I just want to get to him.'

'This is the fastest way,' he promised. 'I know you're angry, but let me do this.'

Emmeline looked away, panic and worry making her uncertain.

Pietro's voice came to her as if from a long way away. He spoke into his phone in his own language, ordering the flight preparations to begin. In some part of her mind she was glad. She was furious with him—furious in a way she doubted she'd ever forgive—but she wasn't sure she could face this completely alone.

He disconnected the call and she spoke without meeting his eyes. 'When?'

'Now. Come. I'll drive.'

She kept her eyes averted as he lifted her suitcase easily, carrying it down the stairs and past the car he'd given her only hours earlier. She ignored the anguish that churned her gut.

Mrs M. What a joke. She'd been nothing to him. Was this why he'd married her? To keep this lie? To deceive her?

All her ideas that their marriage had begun to mean something real were obviously just stupid, childish fantasies. There was no way that he loved her as she loved him. If he'd cared for her at all he would have found a way to break the truth to her sooner.

She stared out of the window as he took the car to Fiumuncino, the countryside passing in a blur that eventually gave way to the built-up cityscape and then more industrial outlying buildings. Finally, it pulled up at a small air terminal.

'Here.' He nodded towards a hangar that was guarded by a single soldier.

It wasn't Emmeline's first time flying in a private jet—her father's was permanently stationed in the States—so it was no surprise for her to be ushered through a private building and customs area before being whisked across the deserted Tarmac to a jet bearing a golden 'M' on its tail.

He handed her suitcase to an attendant, but it wasn't until he climbed the stairs with her that it occurred to Emmeline he might be coming along for the trip. That she might have given herself a rather long flight with a man she never wanted to speak to again.

'What are you doing?' she asked, her words as cold as ice as she paused at the top of the plane's steps.

'What do you think?' He walked deeper into the plane, pausing at an armchair and waiting for her to follow.

She shot him a pointed look, but moved towards him. Fine. If he wanted to join her—to sit with her—then she'd make him sing for his supper. He could damned well give her some answers to the questions that were crashing around inside her.

'So he told you before you and I had even agreed to the marriage?' she said, sitting down in the armchair and buckling her seatbelt in place.

Her fingers were trembling so she clasped them firmly in her lap. Shock was a wave that was spreading around her, swallowing her in its depths.

'He bullied you into marrying me,' she murmured, her eyes locking on the view beyond the window. She had to focus on this conversation or she'd fall apart.

A muscle jerked in Pietro's cheek at her characterisation of their marriage. 'He asked me to help him.'

She pulled a face. 'To help him *manage* me? God! This was meant to be *my* decision. My first step to freedom.'

There was a throb of anxious silence, and if Emmeline had lifted her eyes to Pietro's face she would have seen the aching sympathy there. But she couldn't look at him. His face was now inextricably linked with betrayal.

'He was worried about how you'd cope. He didn't want you to see him unwell.'

Emmeline stared out of the window, the lump in her throat growing bigger by the minute. Was he in pain? Was the housekeeper Miss Mavis looking after him? Was he scared? Tears filled her eyes and she didn't bother to blink them away.

'I didn't agree with his decision, but I had to honour it.'

She whipped her head around, barely able to see him through the fog of her grief. 'Don't *say* that. You can't have it both ways! If you didn't agree with his decision then you should have *told* me.'

'I wanted to tell you.' A frown was etched across his face. 'I'd decided I would tell you one day, when the time was right.'

Her laugh was a harsh sound of fury. 'You just said he has months, maybe weeks, to live. What were you waiting for?'

'Excuse me, *signor*? *Signora*?' An attendant practically tiptoed down the centre of the plane, her expression professional. 'We're ready for take-off. Can I get you anything to eat? Drink?'

'No,' he snapped curtly.

'Yes. Scotch. Neat,' Emmeline demanded. 'And some aspirin.'

'Yes, *signora*.'

Pietro leaned forward and put a hand on her knee once privacy had been restored. 'This changes *niente*— nothing about what we are.'

'Like hell it does!' Her disbelief was a force-field of shock. 'You have been lying to me this whole time. *This whole time.*' She sat back in her seat, all the fight in her evaporating as quickly as it had appeared.

When the attendant appeared with her drink she threw it back, then lifted the aspirin.

'Don't take those,' he murmured. 'You've just had a ton of alcohol…'

She glared at him angrily and tossed the pills into her mouth. 'Go to hell.'

She woke somewhere off the coast of the States. Her head was pounding, her eyes were scratchy and there was a heaviness in her heart that didn't initially make sense. She was disorientated and confused.

She blinked her eyes open and looked forward.

Straight into the brooding stare of her husband.

The smile that was always so quick to come to her lips when she saw him did not come.

Sadness and grief sludged through her instead, and then it all came rushing back. The lie. The secrecy. The betrayal. Her father's cancer.

The fact that he was going to die.

And she hadn't been with him.

Instead she'd been living in Italy, believing everything was amazing, pretending she was normal, truly thinking herself to be happy.

'You told me I could trust you,' she said, so quietly he had to strain to hear the words. 'Do you remember?'

'*Si.*'

'You were talking about Bianca and the other women. But I took it to mean you were generally trustworthy.'

'Your father trusted me,' he said softly, darkly, the words slicing through her resolve.

The betrayal—by both the men she loved—cut her to the quick.

'I can't believe he told you and not me. How dare he? How dare *you*?'

'He was concerned that you would be very vulnerable when he is no longer with us. You will inherit an enormous fortune, and he felt you hadn't had the experience necessary to remain safe from less desirable elements. He wanted to know you were protected. Is that so awful?'

'Yes!' she spat angrily. 'He was afraid of wild dogs and so he sent me to live with a wolf.'

Pietro's eyes flashed with suppressed frustration.

'Don't you *get* it? I will never believe anything you say again. You begged me to trust you and I did. Apparently I was just as naïve and stupid as Daddy thought.'

She glared out of the window, her heart thumping hard when land appeared below. She was back in her country—or the airspace above it, at least—and she never planned to leave it again.

She was home. At least, that was what she told herself.

'Oh, sugar.' Miss Mavis pulled the door inwards, her face lined with tears. Her middle was comfortingly round and she pulled Emmeline against her, holding her tight. 'I'm so sorry.'

Emmeline was aware of everything in that instance. Miss Mavis's sweet scent—like lemon and sugar and butter all rolled into one—the sound of an aeroplane droning overhead, the way Pietro stiffened at her side, and the way her own heart lurched and rolled with the certainty that it was too late.

'I came as soon as I heard. How is he?'

'Oh, Miss Emmeline…'

Miss Mavis's face crumpled and Emmeline knew. She just *knew*. Even the light was different as it glistened across the front of Annersty. The sun was bleak, mourning his loss.

'When?'

The quiet question came from behind her—a voice as much stained by grief as her heart was. And she didn't doubt the truth of his sadness. Pietro had loved Col like a father. Had loved him enough to marry her just to give Col some semblance of reassurance at the end of his life.

'An hour ago,' Miss Mavis sobbed. 'We tried to call you, but your phone…'

Miss Mavis, whom Emmeline had known from five years of age, was like family. She ran a hand over Emmeline's back, holding her tight, comforting her.

'Can I see him?' Emmeline whispered, sounding like the little girl she'd been the year Mavis was hired.

'Of course you can.'

Miss Mavis stepped inwards and Emmeline followed, but then she spun around, her eyes fiercely accusing as they locked to Pietro's.

'Don't.'

She lifted a hand to emphasise her point, then fixed her gaze somewhere over his shoulder. She didn't want to look at the pallor of his face, the haunted eyes. She didn't want to think about the fact that he'd lost someone he loved as well. That he was possibly as wrenched apart by sadness as she was.

'Don't you dare come into my house.'

He flinched as though she'd hit him. *'Cara...'*

'No. Don't you dare.'

Miss Mavis's hand on her back offered strength and comfort. She was feeling more and more like herself again.

'If I'd never married you I would have been with him. *I would have been with him.*'

Pietro braced a hand on the side of the door but otherwise made no effort to move inside. 'It's not what he wanted.'

'He was wrong. *You* were wrong.' She shook her head angrily. 'You should have told me. I should have been here. I'll never forgive you for this.'

She stepped backwards and slammed the door shut, sobbing as it latched into place.

CHAPTER THIRTEEN

ON THE THIRD day after her father died—the morning of the funeral—she found a note stuffed in a book. It had fallen beneath his bed, and she'd pulled it out, was unfolding it slowly, when a knock at his door startled her. She spun guiltily, jamming the piece of paper into her vintage Dior clutch.

Pietro stood in the opening, dressed in a black suit, his dark hair styled back from his face, and he looked so strong and handsome, so supportive and sexy, that she wanted to throw herself across the room and take every bit of strength he was willing to give her.

But she didn't. Because he'd destroyed what they were. Or maybe what they'd never been. The illusion of their marriage seemed like a dream now—one she would never have again. He'd kept his distance since they'd arrived at Annersty, and yet he'd always been there. Dealing with the lawyers, the servants, the mourners who arrived unannounced.

'It's time to go,' he said quietly, his face lined with sympathy and sorrow.

The childish urge to tell him to stay the hell away from the funeral evaporated in the midst of what she knew her father would have wanted and expected. Col had loved Pietro, and she knew her husband well enough to know that it was mutual.

'I'm not going with you.' She settled for that instead.

'Yes, you are.'

He pushed the door shut, leaving him on the bedroom side of it, and walked towards her. She froze like a deer in the headlights—as she had on their wedding night.

She tilted her chin defiantly, remembering all that had happened since that night. Changes had been wrought on her personality and her confidence—changes that couldn't be undone now.

'We *will* go together because if we arrive separately it will cause gossip and scandal.'

'Oh, heaven forbid anyone should cast aspersions on the great Pietro Morelli's marriage—'

'I don't give a damn what the papers say about *me*,' he interrupted firmly, his expression showing grim sympathy, 'but your father, on this day, deserves the focus to be on him. I will not provide the media with any distraction from the greatness he achieved in his long career of public service.'

'Oh, God.' She gripped his shirt for support as her body weakened, a wave of nausea rolling over her at the recognition of what this day was. 'I can't do this.'

'Yes, you can.'

'I can't!' she sobbed, shaking her head from side to side. 'I can't bury him. I can't. *I can't.*'

'Hush…hush.'

He stroked her back, her hair, held her tight, whispered words in his own language—words she didn't try to translate. She didn't need to understand what he was saying to feel comforted.

'I'm here with you.'

And he was. He stayed by Emmeline's side throughout the awful, necessary ordeal. As she said goodbye to the hundreds of lawmakers, donors and friends who'd come to pay their final respects. Pietro's mother and brother were there too, and it was strange to see them here in the church at Annersty. Her new family merging with her old.

Only they weren't her family.

And Pietro wasn't really her husband.

The funeral was a time to say goodbye to more than just Col. It was an ending of all things.

Late that night, when everyone had left and it was just Emmeline and her grief, Pietro found her on her knees in a room that he quickly surmised had been hers as a girl.

'What are you doing here?' she asked without looking, the tone of weary defeat thick in her words.

He crouched down beside her and handed her a mug. 'Coffee?'

She took it, her eyes red-rimmed. 'Thank you.' She curled her fingers around it and sat down on her bottom, staring around the room. 'I was just wishing I could lift a corner of the blanket of time and slip beneath it.' Her smile was vague. 'I want to be a little girl again.'

'The room is very…pink.'

She nodded. 'My favourite colour.'

'I'm surprised,' he said quietly. 'I would have thought perhaps green or red.'

Emmeline wrinkled her nose. 'Nope. Pink. Rainbow. Sparkles.'

She sipped her drink and then pushed herself up to stand, pacing over to the window.

'It was a nice funeral.'

'It was. A fitting service for a man like your father.'

Silence filled the room. A sad, throbbing ache of quiet that spread darkness through Emmeline's soul. She wanted to lift the blanket of time and go back days, not just years. She wanted to be back in Rome, lying in Pietro's arms, hot and slumberous from having made love to him all night, smiling as though the world were a simple place.

But she couldn't go back. Time was a one-way train and it had scooped her up, deposited her on tracks she didn't want to be on. Yet here she was, bound by grief and betrayal, and her destination was fixed.

'There's no point you being here,' she said softly. 'You should go back to Rome.'

'No.' A quiet word of determination. 'I'm not leaving you.'

She turned to face him, her expression blank. 'I don't want you here. Daddy was wrong to think I couldn't cope with this. And he was wrong to think you and he should keep it from me. It's all wrong. Everything we are has been a mistake.'

'It's not the time to make this decision,' he said stonily. 'You have buried your father today.'

'I know what the hell I've done today!' she snapped. 'Tomorrow, the next day—it doesn't matter. Nothing's going to change how I feel.' She sucked in a breath, her lungs burning with hurt. 'If you care about me at all, you'll go. Please.'

His eyes were impossible to read as they locked to hers. He stared at her for a long moment and then nodded softly, turning on his heel and leaving. He pulled the door shut with a soft click but Emmeline was as startled as though he'd slammed it.

Well? She'd been emphatic. What had she expected? That he'd sweep her off her feet and carry her to bed? Lie her down and stroke her back until she fell asleep?

That spoke of an intimacy that had been a lie. How could anything make sense when trust was broken between them? And, no matter what he said or did, he'd broken their trust in the most vital of ways. Robbing her of the chance to be with her father in his last months. To love him and care for him.

She had another sip of coffee, her eyes following the moonlight that danced over the rolling hills of the estate. The trees she'd always loved…the hills she'd rolled down as a young girl.

Strange that she no longer felt the same ties to Annersty she had at one time believed unbreakable. It was no longer the home she saw when she closed her eyes. Instead, her mind was filled with visions of fruit orchards and a tumbling down farmhouse.

She blinked her eyes open, determined not to let her traitorous thoughts go there.

Emmeline slept fitfully, her dreams punctuated by loneliness and grief, her mind heavy with sadness and need. When she woke she was pale, and there were bags under her eyes. She didn't bother to hide them. It was only the housekeeping staff here, and Miss Mavis had seen her in all modes over the years.

Emmeline pulled on a pair of jeans and a sweater. It wasn't a particularly cold day, but she was cold inside.

When Emmeline had finished senior school, and decided not to attend college so she could keep an eye on her father, she'd moved out of her old bedroom and into a larger suite of rooms. It had been more appropriate, given the fact she'd been of an age when most people were moving out of their parental homes for good. She had a large bedroom, a walk-in wardrobe, a beautiful bathroom that had always made her feel as though she was in an old-fashioned book like *Gone with the Wind*, and beyond that a sitting room and office that had a beautiful view over the lake in the East Lawn.

Her eyes were focussed on that window as she crossed the sitting room, seeking out the view that had always provided such a balm to her soul, so it wasn't until she heard a movement that she realised she wasn't alone.

Pietro was on the sofa, scruffy as hell and even more physically beautiful for his air of dishevelment. He wore the trousers from the suit he'd had on at the funeral, and the shirt too. The jacket had been discarded somewhere. He'd pushed his shirtsleeves up and his hair was thick and tousled, as though she'd been dragging her fingers through it all night even though she knew she'd never do so again.

She froze, her eyes unable to do anything but drink him in. To stare at him as though he was the answer to every question that had made her toss and turn all night.

'*Buongiorno.*'

His voice was gravelled perfection. She sucked in a breath, steadying herself, blinking her eyes to clear the image of him as the man she loved. How could she forgive him? He was her father's friend. And a liar.

'What are you doing here?'

He stood, and if she had ever seen him in the boardroom she would have recognised the look of unshakable determination that set his face.

'I'm staying with you.'

'I told you to go.' It was a bleak rejoinder.

The wind ran around the house, wuthering against the walls and shaking the glass behind her. She jumped as it banged loudly in its ancient timber frame.

He stood, crossing the room so that he stood before her. He didn't touch her, but he looked at her so intently that he might as well have.

'I love you,' he said simply. 'If you are here then I am here.'

She made a noise of exasperation. 'You don't need to pretend any more! Daddy's dead. It's over. You did what you were supposed to do. We can let this charade go.'

She wrapped her arms around her chest, hugging herself tight.

If anything, his expression simply assumed an air of even greater determination. 'You need to eat something.'

'I'm not hungry.'

'You look terrible.'

Her eyes flashed with pent-up emotion. 'Just as I did when we first became engaged? This is who I *am*, Pietro. You might have tried the Cinderella treatment on me but I'm just this person. Here.'

It took all his strength not to respond angrily. He *was* angry! Bitterly so. But he smiled gently instead.

'I mean you look like you *feel* terrible. You look as though you haven't slept. You look as though you have lost weight even in the few days we have been in America. Please, come and eat something.'

'This is *my* house,' she said coldly. 'I'll do what I damned well please.'

She stalked out of her suite, her shoulders square, her gaze focussed on the stairs ahead. But her heart was breaking and her eyes were leaking hot, salty tears of misery…

* * *

Days passed in a strange fog. Pietro was always there. Sleeping on the definitely too short sofa just outside her bedroom, keeping his distance but also watching her constantly. After a week she stopped wanting him to go. She stopped wishing he would go. Or rather she began to accept that she was glad he'd stayed.

Her world had been rocked off its axis with Col's death, and having Pietro with her offered comfort that she knew she couldn't get from anyone else. Even Sophie, with her cheery visits and bottles of wine, couldn't erase the throbbing ache deep in her heart.

Emmeline didn't speak to Pietro. Not beyond the obligatory morning greeting and an occasional comment about the weather. But his constant presence was doing something strange inside her. Something she needed and resented in equal measure. She was starting to feel like herself again, and she hated it that it was because of Pietro.

A month after Col's death Emmeline came home to find her father's lawyer in the lounge, locked in conversation with Pietro.

'We've discussed this,' Pietro was saying firmly. 'The estate passes in its entirety to Emmeline.'

Emmeline paused on the threshold, a frown on her face, before sweeping into the room. Pietro's expression was wary, his concern obvious. Emmeline knew why. She had continued to lose weight and she didn't have any to spare.

She ignored his concern and smiled politely at Mr Svenson. 'Can I help you with something, Clarke?'

'Oh…um…er…'

'It's handled,' Pietro said firmly, standing.

Clarke Svenson followed his lead, smiling kindly at Emmeline as he moved as quickly as possible towards the door.

As soon as they were alone, Emmeline whipped around to face her husband. 'What was that all about?'

Pietro expelled a sigh and reached down for his coffee cup. He took a sip and she realised, with a sudden flash of guilt, that he hardly looked his best either. He looked tired, and she hated the way her heart twisted in acknowledgement of the fact.

'There are the usual scum looking to get in on your father's will. Long-lost second cousins twice removed—that sort of thing.' He rolled his eyes. 'It's being handled.'

Her eyes were round in her face. 'By you?'

'*Si*. Someone has to evaluate the claims on their merits.' He moved towards her, slowly, cautiously, as though she were a skittish horse he needed to calm.

She nodded, but without understanding. 'And you've been doing that?'

'*Si.*'

'Why?'

'Because I'm your husband,' he said softly. 'Because you needed me to.'

His eyes ran across her face and he took a step closer, but she shook her head.

'And because my father expected you to,' she added softly.

So much of what they were came back to that, and Emmeline couldn't shake the feeling that she'd been traded. That she was not so much an asset as a bad debt that her father had needed to hand off before he'd died.

Her grief was never-ending.

'We must talk,' he murmured gently.

'I know. But I'm not… I can't… I can't. Not… I'm not…ready.'

'Okay—that's okay. I understand.'

'God, *stop* being so understanding. Stop being so kind. I don't want you here, picking up all these pieces. No matter how kind you are now, nothing can change what happened.'

He ground his teeth together, his eyes clashing with hers. 'I hated lying to you.'

'That's *bull*. You aren't the kind of man who would do anything he hated.'

'It was the perfect rock and a hard place,' he said with understated determination. 'Your father made me swear I wouldn't tell you…'

'How did you think I'd forgive this?' she asked. 'How did you think we'd move past it?'

'I don't know,' he said honestly. 'But I knew we would. I know we *will*.'

'How? How *can* we?'

'Because I am me, and you are you, and together we have found something so special, so unique, that it is irreplaceable.' His eyes forced hers to meet his, and the challenge was impossible to ignore. 'I worried about you not knowing. I worried about you finding out and about you losing your father. I worried about your anger and your hurt. But I never once thought it would be the end for us.'

He stared at her still, his eyes begging her to see, to understand.

'Can you look at me now and think there is a life which we don't share?'

'It was all a lie.' She was numb.

'Nothing about what we are was a lie.'

'Yes, it was! You were my... You woke me up, remember? With you I became a proper, full person. I felt whole and mature, and the most like myself I've ever felt. And really you were just an extension of Daddy. Managing me and infantilising me out of a mistaken belief that I can't look after myself. I thought you saw me as an equal, but instead I was your obligation.'

'At first,' he said, the words a thick concession. 'But you dressed me down at our wedding and I knew that Col was wrong about you. You were naïve, yes, but not weak. Not incapable of handling yourself.'

He reached out and took her hand in his, and his relief at her letting him hold it was immense.

'I'm not here to protect you. I'm here because I need you—and right now you need me. That's marriage.' He stroked the soft flesh of her inner wrist. 'I want more than anything to be married to you. Not because your father sought it, but because of who you are and what we have come to mean to one another.'

The words were like little blades, scraping against the walls she'd been building brick by brick around her heart.

And yet she wasn't ready.

She couldn't forgive him.

'It's too soon. Too much.' She blinked away tears and pulled her hand back to herself. 'If you'd slept with another woman I would find it easier to forgive.'

His laugh was a harsh sound of disbelief. 'You are grieving, and I am trying to give you the space you need. I do not want to crowd you. And I certainly don't want to fight with you. But ask yourself this question: What could I have done differently? I spoke to your father weekly, urging him to tell you about his illness. He was adamant that you should not know.'

'You spoke to him *weekly*?' If anything her sense of betrayal yawned wider.

'He wanted to be reassured you were happy.'

'Oh, *what* a good friend you were!' she snapped, but the indignation of her words was somewhat marred by the sob that strangled them. 'You went above and beyond to make me happy.'

A frown was etched over his handsome face.

'You made it so obvious that you weren't attracted to me, and still you seduced me. You made me think I was *very* happy.'

'None of that had anything to do with your father.'

She rolled her eyes. 'It was *all* because of him. He pulled the strings—just like he did with me my whole life.' She stamped her foot. 'You were supposed to be *mine*. Rome was meant to be *mine*.'

'I didn't marry you with any expectations that it would become a real marriage. That was all *us*. I fell in love with you, Emmeline. Not because of Col but because of you and me.'

The words were sucking her in—so sweet, so exactly what she needed to hear that she rejected them instantly.

'No.'

She held a hand up in the air. To silence him? Or slap him?

'Lying to me about Dad, keeping his secret—that's completely incompatible with love. Love is honesty and truth. It's trust.'

'In a perfectly black and white world, perhaps. But nothing about this was simple. My loyalties were split from the moment I met you. I made him a promise before I even properly knew you. I felt obligated to stick to it. That's the man you love.'

She blinked, felt her heart bricking itself up, its walls forming more easily now they had well-worn foundations.

'I don't love you,' she mumbled tightly. 'I never did. I see that now. I loved Rome. I loved sex. But you? No. I don't even *like* you.'

She spun on her heel and walked quickly from the lounge, waiting until she was in her own room before she let out the sob that was burning inside her.

That night, her dreams were terrifying.

Her mother stood behind Emmeline, her face pinched, dressed all in black.

'See? This is what you deserve, Emmeline. You are alone. All alone. Nobody will be there for you. And that's as it should be.'

It was the crying that woke him. Emmeline had been tossing and turning and crying out in her sleep almost nightly for the whole month they'd been at Annersty. But this was different.

Her sobbing was loud, and when she began to say, 'Go away! Go away! Go away!' again and again in her sleep he felt a cold ache throb through him.

He'd stayed because he'd believed it to be what she needed. But was it possible he was hurting her more with his presence?

I don't even like you.

That was possibly more damning than her insistence that she was angry. It was such a cold denial of all that they were.

Torn between going to her and letting her settle herself, he was just standing to move into her bedroom when she went quiet. All returned to normal.

Pietro took up his cramped space on the sofa, his mind an agony of indecision. Torn between what she needed and what he wanted, he knew there was only one option open to him.

If she needed him to go so she could have the space to realise what they were, then he had to give it to her.

CHAPTER FOURTEEN

EMMELINE STARED AT herself in the mirror with a frown. The dress was beautiful. Her hair was neat. Her make-up flawless.

But she looked wrong. Different. Something was missing. The tan she'd acquired in Rome? The smile that had permanently framed her face? The glint she'd become used to seeing in her eyes—one of utter happiness?

No matter.

She wasn't that girl any more.

She blinked and stepped away from the disappointing image in the mirror. She had no time for maudlin self-reflections. She was late.

Thankfully Sophie was permanently at least fifteen minutes behind schedule, but Emmeline still felt stressed as she lifted her vintage clutch and tucked it under her arm. She pulled her bedroom door inwards, and the lurch of emptiness as she crossed the threshold and stepped into the small area that Pietro had used as a makeshift bedroom was like falling into a pit of quicksand.

There was nothing left of him. Not even the faint hint of citrus and pine that had lingered a day or two after he'd told her he would go if that was what she'd really wanted.

The horrible truth was she *hadn't* wanted that—not really. She'd nodded as he'd said the words, seeing that his mind was apparently made up, but her heart had been screaming. Begging him to stay, willing him to ignore everything she'd said and just be with her.

He'd driven away only an hour after they'd spoken, and the sense of grief and loss had almost eclipsed anything she'd felt since her father had died.

He'd messaged her every second day over the fortnight since he'd left but she hadn't replied. Not because she'd wanted to be childish or to punish him, but because she had no idea what to say. How to express feelings that she couldn't even comprehend herself. The grief, the betrayal, the disbelief. The worry that he'd been pushed into a marriage he'd never wanted. That she'd been falling in love while he'd been making do. The worry that she'd never be able to trust that there had been truth in *any* of their interactions.

She slipped behind the wheel of her car, her expression bleak as she started the engine and began to make her way into town.

The Bowerbird Lounge was doing a roaring trade, despite the fact it was a grey November day. The tables outside featured patrons wrapped in brightly coloured blankets, and the heaters beneath the awnings were on and glowing warm.

As she'd expected, Sophie was nowhere to be seen, but their reserved table was available so Emmeline took a seat and ordered a Diet Coke. She enjoyed people-watching. With her dark sunglasses firmly in place, she gave herself the freedom of scanning the room, watching the guests and catching snippets of conversation.

Ten minutes later her phone began to buzz and she reached into her clutch, pulling it out and answering it when she saw Sophie's face beaming back at her from the screen.

'Hey, hon, I'm just looking for a space. I'll be a few minutes, okay?'

'That's fine,' Emmeline murmured.

'Seriously... What the hell? There's no spaces on this whole damn block.' Sophie made a grunting noise of complaint and Emmeline smiled, tinkering with the clip on her purse.

A piece of the lining, old and fine, ran across her fingertip. She tried to pull it straight, then realised it wasn't the lining at all. It was a piece of paper, folded several times, with her name on the front.

Her heart was pounding so hard and fast that she could no longer hear the din of the restaurant. She disconnected the call and dropped her phone to the table, her fingers shaking as she unfolded the letter. The letter she'd thrust into her bag on the morning of the funeral and forgotten about.

How had she forgotten? Disbelief raged inside her as she sat, ready to read whatever the note contained.

Her dad's handwriting was barely recognisable to Emmeline. It was spidery and fine, weak and pale.

Pumpkin...

Emmeline felt tears sting her eyes. She could hear Col's voice so clearly. She sucked in a deep breath and kept reading.

At the end of one's life I suppose it's natural to re-flect. On choices, decisions, roads not taken. Having you as a daughter is the best thing I've ever done, but I wonder now if I've done it all wrong. Have I failed you? More than likely. That's hard for me to admit, because I have always tried to do everything in my power to make your life a good and rich one.

I didn't want to lose you so I kept you close, and I got in the way of you living your own life. I've been selfish.

These last few months...knowing you to be in Rome, on the brink of so much excitement in your life, so happy with Pietro... I have finally seen you as you should have been all along. Your happiness and independence is the most precious gift I have ever received. I wish I could have helped you find them sooner.

I know my death will have come as a surprise. But while I know you are shocked, you must know that I wanted it this way. Please don't be angry with me for keeping my diagnosis from you. I wanted to spare you as much pain as possible, and I know you would have deferred your own pleasure and adventures to stay close to me. You've done far too much of that already.

Pietro disagreed with my decision, but he was faithful to the last. I am grateful to him for upholding my confidence even when he felt strongly that you would prefer to know the truth. Sparing you the pain of seeing me as I've become is my last gift to you—and it is a gift, Pumpkin. I am not this man.

I hope you can both forgive me for making him stay the course. Or perhaps I have been selfish to the last.

Be happy together. He is a good man and he loves you very much.

As do I.
Forever,
Daddy

Emeline didn't realise she was sobbing until the young girl at the table beside her reached across with a tissue.

'Oh, I'm sorry…'

Emmeline stood up, the table jerking loudly as she moved. She wove through the restaurant and caught Sophie just as she was bursting through the door.

'I have to go,' Emmeline said quickly. 'I'm sorry.'

'Is everything okay?'

Emmeline shook her head, then nodded, her face showing all the confusion that was rich in her heart. 'I… I don't know.'

She handed the letter to Sophie and wrapped her arms around herself as her best friend scanned its contents.

Afterwards, she lifted her eyes to Emmeline's face, trying very hard not to react. 'Where did you get this?'

Emmeline's voice was a sob. 'It was…it was in his book. I found it on the day of the funeral but I… I put it in my clutch and I just found it now. I didn't even think about it again. I suppose I presumed it was just… I don't know. Why didn't I read it sooner?'

Sophie tsked sympathetically. 'Would it have changed anything?'

Emmeline's expression bore anguish. Sophie knew the truth of the situation now—including her real reasons for marrying Pietro.

'How can he have thought it was the right decision?'

Sophie expelled a soft breath. 'Your father was a very proud man.'

'God, I know that. I *know* that! But he was also selfish.' Her voice cracked as she spoke the condemnation. Hot guilt at betraying him spread like wildfire through her body. 'He had *no right* to decide to cut me out.'

'He wanted you to be happy.'

'So he sent me away?'

Sophie sighed. 'Imagine if you'd stayed. You'd have nursed your father and you'd have been by his side when he died, sure. You'd have seen a great, strong man become weak and no longer in control of his body. And when he died you'd have been alone. Bereft. Miserable. Instead you have a new life. A life you love.'

'A life my father *chose* for me,' Emmeline scoffed. 'Don't you *see*, Sophie? I should have been free to find my own way!'

'If you had every choice in the world before you, would you want anything other than what you had with Pietro? Would you have chosen any differently for yourself?'

Emmeline's heart skidded at the mere mention of her husband's name. It spurred an ache deep inside her gut, for it was not just a random collection of letters. It was a call that her body instinctively wanted to answer. It was a promise and a denial. It was everything.

'You can choose now, Emmeline. It's not too late. You have the world at your feet. What do you want to do?'

* * *

Pietro was on fire, and then he was ice-cold. His brow beaded with perspiration as once again he read the letters at the top of the document. Did he miraculously expect them to alter in some way? To rearrange themselves and say something else.

PETITION FOR DIVORCE
Emmeline Morelli v Pietro Morelli

He swore, using every curse he knew, and then repeated them for good measure, scraping his chair back and moving to the door of his office even as he wrenched his phone from his pocket. For the second time in two months he ordered his jet to be made ready at a moment's notice, the urgency in his voice instantly communicating itself to his unflappable assistant.

He stared at the document for the entire drive to the airport, and then again as the plane lifted off. It was a straight-up divorce petition. No dispute over assets or ongoing entitlements, despite his considerable wealth—then again, her own fortune was formidable. She had no need to make a claim on his.

But it bothered him because everything about the document spoke of a woman who wanted to wrap their marriage up swiftly—to bring it to an official conclusion in the fastest possible way.

Did she really think he'd sign the damned thing? Without so much as a conversation?

His plane touched down in the early evening and Elizabetta, with her usual efficiency, had organised a driver to collect him. He stared broodingly out of the window as the car cut through the miles between the airport and Annersty.

But when it pulled up at the front of the grand estate the adrenalin that had brought him the whole way to Georgia seemed to disappear. He swore under his breath and pushed himself out of the car, the divorce papers clutched in his hand.

Miss Mavis answered the door and her smile was warm. Precisely the opposite of what he expected from Emmeline.

He was unable to dredge up more than a grimace of acknowledgement. 'Is she home?'

'Yes, sir.' Miss Mavis stepped back, holding the door wide open. 'She's swimming, I believe.'

'Swimming?' He arched a brow. Well, he hadn't expected *that*.

He stormed through the house, anger taking the place of adrenalin. How dared she end their marriage like this? Without the courtesy of so much as a phone call? Hell, she hadn't even answered his text messages!

As he got closer to the indoor swimming pool the sound of her splashing made him slow. He tried—and failed—to get a grip on his temper. The doors were made of glass. He saw her even before he'd shouldered into the marble-floored room. She was moving slowly through the water, her stroke elegant, her legs languid as they kicked along the length of the pool.

Desire kicked hard in his gut; he forced himself to ignore it.

He ground his teeth together and began to stride on at the side of the water, all the way to the end of the pool. He reached it before she did, and crouched down so that when her fingertips grazed the tiled edge he was able to reach down and touch them. He'd meant simply to alert her to his presence, but the moment he felt her soft flesh beneath his a visceral ache overtook his body—a need to touch more than her fingers, more than her hand.

He straightened in physical rejection of the idea.

She emerged from the water and all he could do was stare at her. Her face was wiped clean of make-up, her hair was slicked back, and her expression showed nothing but shock. He felt something like a stabbing pain in his gut. She was so young, so innocent and so beautiful.

If she wanted a divorce, what kind of bastard was he to fight it? Didn't she deserve her freedom? True freedom? Not the kind that was bargained for and arranged by her father, but the freedom that came of being a young woman who had her own place in the world.

All the fight and the anger he'd brought with him, the disbelief that she wanted to end their marriage, evaporated.

He had to let her go.

He had to do what Col hadn't been able to.

He had to acknowledge that she was a mature woman with every damned right to make her own choices in life.

'Pietro.'

It was a groan and it broke through his resolve. Her eyes dropped to the document in his hands and at the moment of recognition she blanched. Her eyes held desperate anguish as they met his.

'You got the papers.'

'Si, cara.'

Why did she look as though he was killing kittens in front of her? This was *her* choice. *Her* decision.

He looked away, the sight of her making him want more than anything to argue with her. To use any tool at his disposal—yes, even sex—to get her to agree to give their marriage another chance.

But she'd been railroaded enough for a lifetime.

'You didn't have to hand-deliver them.'

Her words were so quiet. So pained. God, how he wanted to swoop down and take that pain away.

'That wasn't my intention.' He stepped back from the water's edge, feeling utter disbelief at what he was about to do.

'Wasn't it?'

The water made a rippling sound as she lifted her arms out of it and braced her forearms against the coping, then pressed her chin into the back of one hand.

'So why *did* you come?'

He shook his head, forcing himself to look at her. But the pain was back—an ache that seemed to rip through him when he met her eyes. The change in her was marked. The happiness that had seemed to shimmer out of her pores in Rome was utterly absent now.

'I was surprised to receive these,' he said, without answering her question.

'Why should you be?'

Visibly, she seemed to tighten her resolve, to assume a mask of unconcern. How did he know it to be a mask? Because he *knew*. He knew everything about her.

'Our reasons for marrying are gone now. He's dead.' Her voice cracked. 'You're free.'

Pietro's head whipped back to hers. He crouched down. Urgency perforated his tone and he spoke before thinking. 'What do you mean, I'm *free*?'

'You did everything he wanted. You were a very

good friend to my father. But it seems only fair to absolve you of this responsibility.'

Now it was Emmeline whose eyes were jerking away, refusing to hold his.

Pietro's mind moved quickly, rapidly sifting through her statement, trying to comprehend her words.

'You're divorcing me because you want to free me from our marriage?' He held the papers up. 'This is for *me*?'

She opened her mouth, surprise obvious in her face. She shook her head, and her eyes showed panic. 'I… It's the right thing to do.'

'*Why* is it, *cara*? Do you think I no longer love you?'

Tears sparkled on her lashes, mixing with the water of the pool. 'Please…don't. Don't say those things. It's not fair.'

His gut whooshed to the floor. She was right. Hadn't he just been telling himself that? And yet…

'I'll sign the papers, Emmeline. If that's what you really want. But I want to hear you say it.'

'Say what?' The words were a whisper and yet they echoed around the pool room.

'Tell me you don't love me.' He crouched down once more. 'Look in my eyes, see all the love I feel for you there, and tell me you don't feel the same.' The words were so deep, so gravelled. 'Tell me you don't want to live in Rome with me, as my wife, that you don't want to be in my bed, that you don't want to continue your studies. Tell me that you want to end our marriage. That *you* want that.'

Her sob was heartbreaking but he didn't withdraw.

'I don't want to be married to you. Not like this.'

Her addendum at the end was a lifeline in the midst of a turbulent, terrifying ocean.

'Not like what?'

'Not because of him. Not because you felt forced to protect me. Don't you see? I'm not the girl he thought I was. The girl *you* thought I was.'

'I know that,' he agreed urgently. 'You never were. I married you because Col asked me to, yes. But I want to stay married to you because of how I feel. How *you* feel. Because of what we *are*.'

Tears ran down her cheeks. She bit down on her lip and looked away from him, trying—and failing—to rally her emotions into order.

'I don't think I believe you.'

The words were agonising to both of them.

'I need us to divorce. It's the only way.'

None of it made any sense. He expelled a soft sigh as he tried to comprehend his wife's viewpoint.

'Then say it.' His eyes held a silent challenge. 'Tell me you don't love me and I'll sign these papers and drop them off at your lawyer's on my way out of town.'

Her sharp intake of breath told him everything he needed to know.

'But if you love me—as I think you do—say that. Tell me that. Be honest with me.'

'Our marriage has no future,' she murmured, ignoring his question. 'I'll never trust you. I'll never believe you're not with me because of a sense of obligation…'

'My God, Emmeline! If this was about obligation do you think I would have slept with you? I tried so hard to fight that, to not want you as I did, and yet you became my obsession. Think about it, *cara*. You had given me *carte blanche* with other women. But I didn't want them. I wanted *you*. I have wanted you from the moment we married. Hell, probably from that moment in my office when you were laying down the ground rules for our marriage.'

She rejected his assertion with a skyward flicker of her eyes. 'Sure. You thought I was so sexy you told me I had to change how I looked.'

He nodded angrily. 'Yes! Because you were so obviously trying to make yourself as uninteresting as possible. And I was right about that. Because even then I knew you. I don't care what you look like, for heaven's sake. I care about how you *feel*. I want you to be happy. I want you to be happy with *me*. But if you want to be here at Annersty alone, or—*God*—with another man eventually, just tell me. Say it and I'll sign these.'

'I can't… I told you. I can't… This marriage…'

He made a sound of frustration, and before she knew what he was doing—perhaps before even Pietro knew himself—he was sliding into the pool beside her, fully dressed. He kicked his shoes off as he wrapped his arms around her waist and drew her to him. And then he kissed her, the surprised 'O' of her mouth giving him the perfect opportunity. He kissed her and she kissed him back.

At least she did for a moment, before her hands lifted to his chest and she sobbed. 'I'll never trust you.'

'Yes, you will.' He stared down at her earnestly. 'I think you already do. I think you hate what happened, and I think you're mad as hell, but I think you love me and you want to find a way to make this work. Do you think that divorcing me will make you happy?'

She stared at him, her expression one of abject fear. And then she shook her head slowly. 'But I need to know you're not trapped. That you're not with me because of him.'

'I'm not.' He arched a brow and pulled her closer, dropping his mouth so that his lips were just a millimetre from hers. 'You gave me a perfect escape clause. You sent me the divorce papers. If I didn't want to be with you do you think I would have flown halfway around the world the second I got them? No. I would have signed them, posted them and heaved a sigh of relief.'

He watched her face, watched it carefully, so that he saw the play of emotions in her features and particularly the moment comprehension seemed to overcome doubt.

'I am *yours*, Emmeline Morelli, for the rest of your life. Married or not, I will never not love you. I will never be with another woman. I will never marry again or have a family. Nothing. Because all that I am…all that I will ever be…is tied up in you.'

Her breath was held in her throat. But still he wasn't sure she understood. So he kissed her again. He kissed her and he whispered into her mouth, over and over and over, like a spell being cast just for her. *'Ti amo, mi amore. Ti amo.'*

In response Emmeline reached up, out of the pool, sliding her fingers across the tiles until they reached the divorce papers. She pulled at them and then, without breaking their kiss, dropped them into the water.

'I love you too.'

'Per sempre?' he groaned.

She nodded. 'Yes. Forever.'

EPILOGUE

Three years later

EMMELINE STOOD IN her graduation robe, clutching her degree, a beaming smile on her face. In the front row sat Pietro, so handsome, so beautiful, and beside him Rafe, Ria and Sophie. Emmeline smiled down at them, waving her fingers as Pietro snapped a photograph, then moved off-stage.

Three blissful years, a university degree, and now she was on the cusp of a life that was about to change forever.

There was a swirling sense of celebration and she took part in all of it—smiling through the after-party, making polite conversation with the university professors who had been so helpful to her.

Finally, though, she was alone with her husband.

'I have something for you,' he said, with obvious pride.

'I have something for *you*,' Emmeline repeated. 'Let me go first?'

'Certo.' He grinned. 'Though it hardly seems fair. You are the one who graduated with distinction today. Surely the gifts should all be for you?'

'My gift is a present to me, too.'

She reached into her bag and pulled out an envelope, handing it to him. She watched as he lifted the flap and then looked at the front of the card. It was just a generic *I love you* gift card she'd picked up at the pharmacist. Nothing special.

But when he opened it to read the contents inside, and lifted his eyes to her face, she saw his shock and surprise and she laughed.

'This says we are going to be parents.'

'I know. I wrote it.'

His jaw dropped and he read the card again, his eyes scanning it over and over just to be sure.

'Are you serious?'

'Uh-huh.'

'But…when?'

Emmeline laughed. 'I think we've given ourselves plenty of opportunities, don't you?'

'We're going to be *parents*.'

He closed his eyes, and when he opened them they were swimming with emotion. He dragged her against his chest and kissed her, and she kissed him back, her heart soaring with love and optimism.

What they were—who they'd become—had taken a leap of faith, a mountain of trust and all the courage Emmeline possessed. And it had been worth it.

She stood in the arms of the man she adored, knowing without doubt that they would live happily. *Per sempre.*

* * * * *

#3621 DESERT PRINCE'S STOLEN BRIDE
Conveniently Wed!
by Kate Hewitt

To reclaim his country, Zayed *must* wed. He steals away his intended...only to realize shy Olivia is the wrong woman! But with such heated chemistry between them, do they want to correct their mistake?

#3622 HIRED TO WEAR THE SHEIKH'S RING
by Rachael Thomas

As Jafar's temporary wife, Tiffany is perfect. Yet this convenient arrangement for his crown leads to passion! Is their craving enough to make Tiffany more than just the sheikh's hired bride?

#3623 SURRENDER TO THE RUTHLESS BILLIONAIRE
by Louise Fuller

Luis is shocked to learn the beautiful stranger he spent one scorching night with has also been hired by his family! He whisks Cristina away to uncover her ulterior motive...and rekindles their incendiary desire!

#3624 PRINCESS'S PREGNANCY SECRET
One Night With Consequences
by Natalie Anderson

Damon can't resist a sensual encounter with a captivating guest at a royal masquerade. But he's shocked to discover she was actually Princess Eleni—and now she's carrying his baby!

Get 2 Free Books,
Plus 2 Free Gifts —

just for trying the Reader Service!

"We were so hot, Cecelia, and we could have been
good, but you chose to walk away. You left. And then
you denied me the knowledge of my child and I hate you
for that." And then, when she'd already gotten the dark
message, he gave it a second coat and painted it black. "I
absolutely hate you."

"No mixed messages, then?" She somehow managed
a quip but there was nothing that could lighten this
moment.

"Not one. Let me make things very clear. I am not
taking you to Greece to get to know you better or to see
if there is any chance for us, because there isn't. I want

no further part of you. The fact is, you are my daughter's mother and she is too young to be apart from you. That won't be the case in the near future."

"How near?"

Fear licked the sides of her heart.

"I don't know." He shrugged. "I know nothing about babies, save what I have found out today. But I learn fast," he said, "and I will employ only the best, so very soon, during my access times, Pandora and I will do just fine without you."

"Luka, please…" She could not stand the thought of being away from Pandora and she was spinning at the thought of taking her daughter to Greece, but Luka was done.

"I'm going, Cecelia," Luka said. "I have nothing left to say to you."

That wasn't quite true, for he had one question.

"Did you know you were pregnant when you left?" Luka asked.

"I had an idea…"

"The truth, Cecelia."

And she ached now for the days when he had been less on guard and had called her Cece, even though it had grated so much at the time.

And now it was time to be honest and admit she had known she was pregnant when she had left. "Yes."

Don't miss
CLAIMING HIS HIDDEN HEIR
available May 2018 wherever
Harlequin Presents® books and ebooks are sold.

www.Harlequin.com

HARLEQUIN
Presents®

Coming next month—Lucy Monroe's latest Harlequin Presents story!

In *Kostas's Convenient Bride*, Kayla's boss needs to marry. Can she step out of the shadows and down the aisle?

Discovering that her boss, billionaire tycoon Andreas Kostas, must marry is devastating for Kayla. Then Andreas proposes that *Kayla* wear his ring! Having experienced the incandescent pleasure of his touch, she's hidden her yearning for him ever since. It's the proposal Kayla's always dreamed of, but does she dare risk her body and her heart to become a convenient wife?

Kostas's Convenient Bride

Available May 2018